Believe Me

Molly Garcia

Contents

I really don't think I would've continued my writing journey if it wasn't for the support and encouragement of my family. It's amazing how they all continue to believe in me even when I'm finding it hard to believe in myself.

Prologue

2008

C arrie Martins held the crumpled shopping list in one hand, while she carefully placed the items in the basket she had hooked over her other arm.

Milk. Hmm, full fat or semi-skimmed? Had her dad specified? She didn't remember him telling her which one. Grabbing a full-fat she laid it gently in the basket before moving along to the next aisle. Eggs joined the milk, as did a loaf of medium white sliced bread, and a jar of raspberry jam.

The shop was busier than she'd usually like it to be. Carrie tried to time her trips for the quieter times when she was less likely to bump into people who wanted to distract her. Since starting work as a teaching assistant at the local primary school she'd found it even worse, parents were constantly stopping her to get informal feedback on their kids. Carrie often longed to be bluntly honest with some parents. "Sorry to tell you this, but little Bobby is way behind the rest of his class and no one likes him."

She smiled to herself at the thought of the reaction she'd get to a bold, blunt statement like that. Carrie was pretty sure most parents didn't really want honest feedback no matter how often they claimed otherwise. Spotting a familiar face heading into her aisle, Carrie speed-walked to the next one where she wouldn't be drawn into an unwelcome conversation.

Despite the number of people milling around the store, there was an unusually subdued atmosphere. Most of the conversations she overheard related to the three missing children from town as everyone speculated on what might have happened to them.

Carrie leaned over the stack of shiny red apples and contemplated getting some. They weren't on her list but they did look really nice. She picked one up and as she was about to take a closer look a firm hand clamped down on her forearm. The apple dropped, any thoughts of buying it forgotten as Carrie spun around to find herself face-to-face with a grim-faced police officer.

Her basket slipped from her arm tumbling in slow motion as it spilled out its contents. The carton of milk exploded sending violent splashes of white to join the bright yellow yolks of her eggs and the dark red sticky jelly of a smashed jar of raspberry jam. Carrie stared at the mess, her head bowed forward by the officer who was busy handcuffing her arms behind her back as he brusquely read her, her rights. Every customer in the shop had turned to watch and she was sure if she looked up they'd have matching expressions of disgust.

The officers were none too gentle as they dragged her outside to the car that was waiting for her, and as the doors slid open to let them out of the shop she heard the starting hum of voices, just before they closed again behind her.

Chapter One

Dr Quinn looked up at the imposing red brick building in front of him and the discreet sign that let visitors, staff, and prisoners know where they were.

HMP Chartridge

The gloomy sky and dark rain clouds created the perfect backdrop giving the whole scene a feeling of impending doom. Pushing those fanciful thoughts away he dug in his pocket and pulled out the ID badge he'd been issued before officially starting in his new post.

Security was as rigid as he'd expected. A notice by the intercom system directed him to press 1 for reception and to look up at the camera tucked under the eaves. The red light at the base of the camera blinked rapidly as someone inside scrutinised the image, clearly satisfied with what they saw Ethan heard a buzz followed by a click and a tinny voice instructing him to push the door.

Reception may have suggested a warm and welcoming environment. However, the reality was a small drab room, the magnolia walls lined by metal benches. To his right, a bulky bored-looking man in a prison guard's uniform sat behind a pane of wire-threaded glass. Ethan passed his ID badge through the slot and the guard flicked his eyes between it and his face as he made sure the photo and the person in front of him matched.

Turning around and reaching behind him, the guard unhooked an alarm and a key and passed them back through to Ethan along with his ID badge.

"I'm going to need you to stow everything in your designated locker please Doc."

Ethan frowned, in his previous roles staff kept their possessions in the staff room lockers accessible during the day so phones could be checked during breaks. He also needed some of the items in his bag, his laptop, his notebooks, and pens for example. He'd known it might be a bit different in a prison to a secure hospital but it did feel a little over the top considering he was a member of the staff team.

Seeing his hesitation the guard explained.

"It didn't used to be this strict, but we had a couple of incidents where staff took items onto the wings that disclosed confidential or personal information, and another where someone left the facility with confidential notes. As a result, there was a policy change and now everyone must leave everything here in their locker. You'll be supplied with everything you need inside, but it must remain there after you leave for the day."

Ethan nodded in agreement before taking the key and working out which locker it corresponded to. Finding number 68 he opened it, and pushed his bag inside. Before he could lock it the security guard called over to him.

"Sorry Doc, but that includes your coat. You can't take anything in there apart from your badge, alarm, mobile phone, and locker key."

Hoping there wasn't too much outside walking to be done on his way to the ward he was designated to Ethan shrugged off his coat and added it to the locker. Clipping the alarm to one of the belt loops on his trousers he followed the arrows over to the metal door at the rear of the room.

The guard pressed a button and the door clicked allowing Ethan to pull it open. Saying a hasty goodbye and thank you to the guard he stepped out into a paved courtyard.

Ethan shivered as he speed-walked over to a large gate where another guard stood waiting for him. This one was a short woman, hefty and grim-faced she made an intimidating welcome party of one.

"Hello Dr Quinn, I'm Bee Croft. I'll show you to the admin block."

Unclipping a large bunch of keys from her uniform she unlocked the gate and held it open for him to go through. Without any further conversation, she led him to a blue reinforced door where she rummaged through her keys until she found the one she needed.

Ethan found himself in a small tiled room, a bank of lifts was on his right next to a door that led to the emergency stairs. Ahead of them was a corridor and a sign indicated that it led to the staff restaurant and restroom.

Bee waved a hand in the general direction of the corridor.

"Self-explanatory, down there are all the staff facilities."

Clearly, a woman of few words, thought Ethan as she used her ID badge to activate the lift. The door slid open immediately and they both squeezed inside the compact space. This close to Bee he could smell the nicotine on her breath and the fluorescent lighting unkindly illuminated the pockmarks on her doughy face.

The doors opened onto another plain white corridor the mirror image of all the others. Bee pointed down the corridor towards a row of white doors that would've merged into the walls if it wasn't for the silver handles.

"Your office is down there, maintenance put up your name plaque yesterday so you'll know which one it is."

Turning slightly she now pointed to a large wooden framed door with the same wire-threaded glass as the security office downstairs. A sign outside proclaimed it to be "Robin Wing" with a small picture of the bird underneath.

"As you can see that's the door that leads to the wing you'll be assigned to. Doctor Edwards is expecting you in his office and he'll give you the guided tour and issue you with your own set of keys. Security wise the only hard and fast rule apart from the obvious is that you can't take your mobile phone onto the wings. I won't be doing this every day, you'll be letting yourself in and out from now on."

Ethan felt a wave of relief that he wouldn't be expected to be in this blunt woman's company on a regular basis but hid it under a friendly smile.

"Thanks, Bee, I really appreciate your help."

"It's Croft not Bee. I don't sit comfortably with all that informality like using a person's first name until you're invited to."

Ethan was suitably rebuked and managed to blurt out an apology before Bee spun on her heel and disappeared back into the lift.

Guessing that Dr Edwards's office would be one of the white doors at the opposite end, Ethan headed in that direction. Each door had a small plaque that told you what it was used for. Dr Edwards's office was towards the end of the corridor. Ethan's knock was answered by a gruff voice that told him to come in. Dr. Edwards was sitting behind a huge desk that was stacked with so many files and folders that the precarious piles almost hid him from view.

He stood up and held out his hand.

"Welcome Dr Quinn, welcome. So good to have you on board. We've been desperate to recruit a doctor specific for the complex needs on Robin Wing for some time."

Ethan shook hands with him, the small, bald man had an unexpectedly firm grip, his papery skin rubbing against Ethan's as he clutched onto his hand.

"So, May Chambers, our resident RMN, will be on shift for you to meet later but in the meanwhile, I'll allocate your caseload and issue you with your own set of keys. After that, you'll need to arrange appointments to meet your patients for their first one-to-ones. We expect each one to meet with you weekly as a minimum but outside of that you'll be able to set your own schedule based on your assessment of their individual needs."

Frowning at the piles of files as though confused about how they got there he finally settled on the smallest stack of seven folders that he picked up and passed to Ethan.

"This is your caseload, we'll sit down and talk about each one after you've read them. This one, however, I feel needs further explanation before you look at it."

Scratching his chin thoughtfully he tapped the folder on the top of the pile to indicate which one he meant.

"Carrie Martins. The name might already ring a bell, she was all over the news in 2008."

Dr. Edwards paused to allow Ethan time to think about it, the name was definitely familiar, he thought, but he couldn't pull up the reason why.

"Maybe you'll recall the name the media gave her during the trial? The Child Catcher."

That name conjured up the lurid headlines of fifteen years ago, Ethan had been a 26-year-old recently qualified psychiatrist at the time. Like many others he'd been morbidly fascinated with the case, wondering how a young woman could brutally murder three children.

These were children she'd known, children who would've trusted her, hence the name "Child Catcher."

To his colleague, he gave a slow nod and kept the enthusiasm and excitement he felt at having her on his list out of his voice and off his face.

"Yes, I do remember. She was only twenty at the time I believe. Did they ever work out her motive?"

Dr. Edwards shook his head and shrugged.

"Not a scooby. Her lawyers tried to use the unfit to stand trial card, but as she wasn't floridly unwell it never panned out and she was sent here instead. We soon found her to be a disruptive influence in general population so she was moved to the vulnerable wing and here she's stayed. She's up for parole and the board wants a full report before making a decision to release her on licence. That's where you come in."

"So, she's never disclosed why she did it, not in all these years? Surely she shouldn't be released if she hasn't accepted what she did?"

His colleague pulled a face and then explained why.

"That's part of what I needed to talk to you about. Carrie is a pathological liar and a fantasist. She'll rarely tell you the truth about anything, not what she ate for lunch and certainly nothing as important as why she's here. Like her other doctors before you, there'll be times when you think you're about to make a breakthrough. Carrie will encourage your optimism, she's manipulative and persuasive, but as soon as you get too complacent she'll back-peddle and change her whole narrative. She's quite possibly one of the most challenging prisoners here. As doctors, we all want to feel as though we're heading towards a positive outcome, but you'll never find any with Carrie Martin. I don't want to prejudice your report before you've even started but I want you to be aware of what you're dealing with. If Carrie gets her parole

I want to be damn sure we won't be dragged into a scandal when she re-offends."

Far from putting him off Ethan's enthusiasm was growing with Dr Edwards's warning lecture. There was nothing he enjoyed more than a challenge, many of his previous patients had been written off as too entrenched in their illness to recover yet he'd found with perseverance and patience he'd managed to achieve small positive outcomes for them.

Dr. Edwards must've read his thoughts across his face because he gave his younger colleague an eye roll.

"And I believe I've just encouraged rather than deterred you. Your enthusiasm and tenacious approach are qualities that we look for here at Chartridge, but in this case, you do need to be realistic about your chances of any level of success. Above all, please keep the risks in mind. If Carrie is released, even on licence, we need to be as certain as possible that she's ready and doesn't pose a risk to the community."

Ethan nodded his agreement while managing to straighten his face into a serious, professional expression that seemed to reassure Dr. Edwards enough for him to move on.

"We've allocated you Carrie Martin because we feel a new face will do her good. She's bored, and when she's bored her risk increases. Carrie likes to entertain herself by manipulating the other prisoners on her wing and being unresponsive to the staff who try to work with her day to day. If she believes she's got a new doctor to work on her engagement might improve. It won't be positive engagement, with Carrie it never is, but at least it'll mean she's more manageable for the staff team."

Dr Edwards took a quick peek at his watch and sighed before pushing a bunch of keys over the desk towards Ethan.

"The days are never long enough! These are your keys, guard them with your life while you're on duty and hand them to security when you leave the building. First things first, take those files along to your office and have a read. In about two hours May will arrive and I'll leave you in her capable hands for the introductions. I'm the senior clinician and as such will be your mentor and line manager."

• • • ● ● • ● ● • • •

May Chambers was a tall woman with wild blonde curls that she'd tried to tame into a messy bun. Bangs had escaped the bright red scrunchie and framed a pleasant oval face that housed a pair of intense blue eyes further magnified by a pair of dark-rimmed glasses. Smiling up at him she told him how relieved she was to finally have a doctor allocated to the wing.

"Dr Edwards has been doing his best, but he's responsible for the whole prison and Robin Wing needs a lot more input than he can offer. The main issue is Carrie Martin, she's such a negative presence. Sounds appalling I know, but I just can't gel with her at all. Partly it's what she's done, but mostly it's the way she is. Cold, manipulative, and lying at every turn, how do you build a positive relationship with someone like that?"

Ethan shrugged, "People like Carrie are some of the hardest we have to work with, especially those who've killed or harmed children."

May nodded briskly clearly pleased he agreed with her.

"Please call me May, at least when we're out of earshot of the prisoners anyway."

"And you must call me Ethan with the same conditions of course."

They shared an amused look before May swept him off in the direction of the wing. Using her ID badge she let them both in, gesturing Ethan to go first while she made sure the door was fully closed behind them. It led to a long corridor, at one end there were rows of small glass-fronted rooms.

"Those are the interview rooms, it's where you'll take the prisoners you're working with for 1:1 chats. A guard will wait outside and make sure you're safe at all times."

At the end of the long corridor was another heavy locked door, this one required a key to access it. On the other side, the layout wasn't what he'd been expecting. Instead of floors and floors of cells, this was laid out more like a hospital environment. Laminated flooring to make it easy to clean, plain magnolia walls, and the staff's station central so they could see everything from inside. The office had the typical goldfish bowl windows that stretched right around the space.

One woman was pacing up and down throwing the occasional glare in the direction of the office. May walked over and made sure she could see her before she spoke.

"Terry, are you okay? Is there something you need?"

The woman turned slowly in her direction, her hand still raised and ready to restart the repetitive tapping on the office window.

"Don't wanna talk to you Miss, go away. You're one of them, talking about me and watching me."

May tried to give the agitated woman a reassuring smile but she'd already looked away and was again pacing up and down. May shrugged and one of the staff unlocked the office door to allow them in. Ethan was introduced to everyone, but he was sure he wouldn't remember everyone's names. They were a blur of uniformed prison officers with one or two wearing civilian clothing like himself and May. It turned out they were support workers who tried to give as many of the unwell prisoners on the wing some time as possible.

It appeared this was going to be a flying visit as when they were offered a coffee May shook her head and refused on behalf of the both of them. Once outside she explained that she had a full afternoon of appointments and felt that he should be spending his first day getting to grips with the files rather than hanging around on the wing.

"They'll keep you there as long as possible if they can, and I can't blame them. As you saw with Terry, the prison is expected to manage prisoners with significant mental health needs, way beyond what they should be coping with. It means there's a high turnover of staff. People leave and they aren't replaced. Even when we get a good response to the ads either they aren't suitable or they don't last more than a week. It's a tough job and only a certain type of person can do it."

Ethan made a mental note. Not because he'd be avoiding it, but rather because he planned to put aside some time each day to spend supporting the staff if he could.

Chapter Two

E than had started meeting with his caseload first thing on his second day. He'd got to grips with their histories and on the whole most of them were exactly what he'd expect from a prison hospital wing. He'd left Carrie Martins until last as he wanted to allow himself as much time as he needed to start relationship-building with her.

His boss's warning had achieved nothing more than to raise his interest in the case. Ethan had written several papers over the years on the subject, "Unreliable life narrators" being his most well-known among his peers. He'd found it fascinating that some people were so skilled in burying the truth among so many lies that most listeners wouldn't bother to dig deep enough to find it.

He'd spent the night before doing an internet search on the original case. Although the files contained all the dry details he felt it wouldn't hurt for him to get a feel of how it had unfolded at the time. The headlines were typically salacious, they'd started with the girls going missing and then really exploded when Carrie was publically arrested in the local supermarket while doing her weekly shop.

She was twenty years old and a teaching assistant at the local prima-ry school. A mousey, quietly spoken young woman whom the children had adored. As was often the case, there were a few people who'd told the press that they'd always thought there was something amiss with Carrie. No names next to the quotes and nothing that would've led anyone to suspect she was capable of murdering anyone, let alone three children. The whole town had been in shock at the news of her arrest. Shock, that had quickly turned to anger when she wouldn't tell anyone why she'd done it. It hadn't helped that by the time her trial started Carrie had completely changed her image. Gone was the mousey hair and loose-fitting clothes, as she walked into the court-room the reporters described an audible gasp from the on-lookers. Carrie's hair was now a glowing honey blonde, her makeup expertly applied and her red dress clung to every curve as though she was about to go clubbing.

Instead of looking nervous, frightened, or even full of remorse, Carrie walked with a confidence that people said they'd never seen from her before. Her heels clacked on the hard floor and her face was set in an expression that suggested this was all below her. The photos made for great journalism the next day. She looked less like a librarian and more like Myra Hindley, a comparison that wasn't missed by the media.

The same question in the lurid headlines also popped into Ethan's head.

Which one was the real Carrie Martin?

Dowdy teaching assistant or the femme fatale we saw in court today?

The unemotional documentation of the murders in her file hadn't entirely taken the horror out of what had happened to those poor children. reading it in the press, however, really brought it home to Ethan.

Three seven-year-old children, two girls, and a boy, had gone into the woods with Carrie one day and never come back out. For a week the police had searched everywhere without finding them. Their sobbing parents had appeared on screens across the country begging for information on their whereabouts, but it wasn't until Dave Everett returned from his holidays and saw it that he stepped forward with some vital information. He'd been walking his dogs when he'd seen Carrie Martin herding three children across the field and into the woods. He'd assumed it was something to do with school and hadn't thought much of it until he'd come back and seen they were missing.

The police had immediately filled the woods with uniforms and sniffer dogs. No child had been found, but there was one little red shoe that matched the ones worn by Tessie Connor the day she'd gone missing. Blood found inside it matched Tessie's DNA and Carrie was quickly arrested and taken in for questioning.

Interesting that the blood, the shoe, and the witness seeing her taking the children into the woods had been enough to charge her, thought Ethan.

There was no sign of the other two children, Thomas Jones and Emily Little. The jury deliberated for barely a couple of hours before handing down the guilty verdict that had seen her taken to HMP Chartridge.

Glancing at the large wall clock he realised Carrie would be on her way to the little room designated for their 1:1. He felt a small buzz of anticipation at his first meeting with her. Unprofessional he knew, but he couldn't help it. Footsteps echoing down the corridor announced her arrival and he turned to look at the door waiting for his first sight of the notorious "Child Catcher"

Her hair had returned to the mousy brown of her teaching assistant days, and she was dressed casually in jeans and a plain blue shirt.

Her black plimsols squeaked on the tiled floor, and she clenched and unclenched her hands nervously as she approached the spare chair. The two guards supervised her until she was seated, before reminding Ethan that they'd be right outside if he needed their assistance. As soon as the door closed he opened his mouth to introduce himself but Carrie overspoke him.

"I know. You're Dr. Ethan Quinn. Newest psychiatric doctor on the wing and the author of "Unreliable Life Narrators.""

Sensing she was looking for a reaction he ensured that he didn't reward her with one, instead, he shrugged and agreed with her.

"That's me in a nutshell, and of course, I already know who you are too."

Carrie smirked, "The Child Catcher."

Ethan continued as though she hadn't spoken, he wasn't sure what she wanted to hear in response so felt it was better to keep things moving. It felt as though she'd thrown that in for shock value and he'd found it best not to feed into it.

"I expect you're wondering what format our meetings will take."

Carrie shrugged, "You'll want me to tell you all about what you think I did, in the hopes that you'll be the first person to get a confession from me. You're already dreaming about the paper you'll write, maybe even a book, and how it'll be the key to fame and fortune."

She yawned as though already bored by the session, but the glint of interest in her eyes wasn't lost on Ethan. Carrie was clearly enjoying the back-and-forth challenge of trying to best him.

He gestured at the camera in the corner of the room, "I'll be filming our sessions. Partly to protect both you and me as we'll be alone in this room, but also so I can watch it back and try and find an approach that works for you."

She barely gave the camera a glance, "As you can imagine, I'm very used to being watched."

"I'm sure you are. Okay, so, I like to start at the beginning, which means talking through your history. Let's start with your first memory."

Carrie sighed, "So very Freud. Surely I should be on a therapist's couch while you ask me in a deadly serious voice to "Tell me about your childhood.""

Ethan leaned back in his chair and let the silence hang for a moment, he often found even the most reluctant of patients would want to fill that gap. Carrie gave him a knowing smile as though unconcerned but he was sure he saw a fleeting look of anxiety on her face. It was gone so quickly he couldn't be certain that he hadn't imagined it. The silence grew uncomfortable, and in the end, he had to break it himself.

"Is that something you find difficult to talk about Carrie?"

She shook her head, "Not at all. Where do you want me to start?"

Ethan steepled his fingers and rested his chin on his hands, "Wherever you feel comfortable starting from."

Chapter Three

Carrie

I have some flashes of memories from my earliest years. I'm not sure if these are genuine or if they come from photos I've seen, but there's nothing especially solid to tell you. I recall eating a huge ice cream on a beach, it was hot and sunny and it was running down the cone and making my hands sticky. I was crying because I didn't like it and my dad was angry that my tears were spoiling our day out.

My dad's an impatient man, always quick to pick me up on my faults and tell me where I'm going wrong. My mum on the other hand was a kind woman, full of love and quick to offer physical affection. She died when I was seven, so I have very few tangible memories of her, but those I do have are pleasant, warm, and loving. Reading me bedtime stories and putting a plaster on my knee when I fell down. I'm an only child, my mother wasn't a well woman and my dad's always said she couldn't have any more children. They didn't think they'd have children at all so I was like the unexpected miracle.

It was just me and my dad after she died. He did his best, even though it must've been hard to raise a child, especially a daughter, alone. He went to every parent's meeting at school, he made sure I always had a clean, ironed uniform and he sat with me while I did my homework. I know I make that sound as though it was just the basics, but he wasn't cold, just a man who found physical demonstrations difficult. He liked his home to be just so, and I often found it hard to live up to his expectations. Don't get me wrong, he loves me, it's just that he has a hard time showing me that he does.

I think one of my clearest early memories is starting school. Standing outside the huge gates, wearing a uniform two sizes too big that my dad believed I'd grow into I clutched his hand. I remember crying as one of the teachers pulled me away from him and I remember handing him a picture I'd painted when he came to collect me later that day. School was difficult for me, I felt different from the other children and I think they sensed it because they gave me a wide berth. I'd spend most of my break time reading by myself or later playing with the younger children.

I was bright, I could read before I started school and I found the lessons easy. Maybe that's why the other children hated me? Who knows. No one invited me to go on play dates and I didn't have anyone to invite home either. Sometimes it was a lonely life, just me and my dad, but mostly it was okay. It was all I was used to and having his attention one-on-one was nice, it's probably why I read at such a young age. He'd sit with me every night reading me stories and helping me to learn the words. I was very lucky to have a father who cared so much, and if he could sometimes be a little distant, well you can't have everything.

I imagine you're hoping for something salacious or terrible in my past that might explain everything to you, but I'm afraid there's nothing. I had a boring, ordinary childhood. The only trauma was losing my mother, but I'm not the first, or sadly the last child, to lose a parent too soon. I'm not a monster, I'm not the Child Catcher they christened me. I'm just an ordinary woman from an ordinary home.

Until I was arrested barely anyone noticed me, but of course, since then I've become notorious.

Chapter Four

Ethan hadn't spotted any obvious tells that she was lying, but he had noticed the inconsistency of claiming her mother was wonderful, and yet it was her father who took her to school on her first day. Her mum didn't die until she was seven, so why was she missing from that important milestone? He was aware from her notes that she was known to weave together the lies and the truth into a story that would be difficult to pick apart. Her expression didn't give him any clues either, she was looking as he'd expect someone to look who'd just shared something personal. A little uncomfortable and awkward, but nothing that suggested deep distress or a psychopath's ability to fake emotional responses. Ethan had also picked up on the last thing she'd said. It'd felt as though she was almost proud of her notoriety and was making sure he was aware of it. A lot of prisoners put a high store in their reputations and maybe this was just something that she used to keep herself safe. If that was the case, then Carrie would soon have found out it wasn't a great idea. Women prisoners in particular had a deep-seated loathing for those convicted of harming children. Many of them were separated from their own kids and were prone to being very hostile to a woman who hurt them.

A glance at the clock told him their time was up, and he could already see the guards getting ready to come and collect her. He checked she was okay and when she nodded told her he'd see her again tomorrow. Watching her back as she walked out into the corridor he wondered how long it'd take to peel back the layers and find the real Carrie, or if he ever would. Heading to his office he downloaded the digital copy of the video and watched it back. He often found it useful to do this after a session as he could focus more on the person's expression and even pause or zoom in if he saw something interesting.

Ethan was especially interested in any micro-expressions she made when talking about the loss of her mum or the difficulties with her father. Pulling out a notebook and pen he made notes of each part.

Talking about mother's death – some rapid blinking and fidgeting.

Talking about Father – Becomes still, almost watchful. Eyes widen slightly.

Why did Dad take and collect her from school on her first day? Was mum already sick or was she not being entirely honest about her mother?

Leaning back in his chair he stared at the paused image. Carrie couldn't be described as beautiful, but at the same time, he wouldn't say she was plain either. She had an interesting face, he mused, and the years had been kind. She hadn't aged too badly in the last fifteen years considering she'd been in prison so long. It wasn't a face ravaged by guilt either, was that because she was a psychopath who didn't care a less? Opening her file he tried to patch together what she'd told him with her records but it was sparse on background and mostly focused on her offences and her time in custody.

"Knock, knock."

May's smiling face looked around the door at him, "You look engrossed, I'd bet my last pound coin that you've just met the enigma that is Carrie Martins."

Ethan waved her in, "Actually it'd be good to talk to someone about her."

May looked at the frozen image on the screen, "I'm not sure I'll be that helpful really. I've been here for nearly ten years now and I still can't tell when she's lying or telling the truth, to be honest, I'm not sure even *she* knows the difference anymore."

She took a seat opposite him and gave him the look that suggested she was about to impart some advice he might not want.

"Ethan, I appreciate that you're fascinated with her case, and I can absolutely see why. The thing is, you won't get any further than anyone else. Just focus on writing up that report and make sure the community is protected from her if they need to be. Personally, and my opinion shouldn't sway your outcome, I wouldn't want her living in my street let alone next door to me. Would you?"

Ethan gave that some serious thought, she did have a point, and it prompted him to look at it from a less therapeutic angle and be practical.

"I don't have children myself, but my sister does. What you're saying did make me think if I'd want her living next door to my nieces."

May shrugged, "It's something to keep in mind when you feel yourself being sucked into the rabbit hole of her carefully woven fantasies."

He felt a spark of annoyance, she might be trying to help but it felt as though she was questioning his ability to see through a patient's lies and fabrications. Pushing aside his irritation he gave a nod of agreement.

"Absolutely May, my only aim is to find out what her level of risk is and to advise the parole board accordingly."

He'd thought he'd hidden his feelings but he could see from her suddenly closed expression she'd picked up on it. May stood and headed for the door before turning to offer him one last piece of advice.

"I know you think you've got it all under control, and I'm not trying to undermine your experience, but Carrie is a master of manipulation. Just be on your guard at all times is all I'm saying."

Ethan looked at the back of the door she'd closed behind her when she left. Deep down he knew he was being sucked in more than he should be, but it was an interesting case. Besides, he told himself, how can you do a report if you don't learn as much about her as you can?

Slowly gathering his files and paperwork together and locking them in his drawer he got ready to leave. Carrie was intriguing him in a way that no other patient had for a long time. He'd been in this job for most of his adult life and the novelty had worn thin a while ago. Still, he'd been happy to plod along in the well-paid position in a private mental health facility. The money kept him and his wife in a lifestyle that didn't involve her working and he was just waiting for the day when they had children. His life had felt all mapped out for him, but his complacency had left him blind to what was really happening.

Never one to shrug off a stereotype, Andrea had been shagging the gardener. And not only him, she'd also been boffing the young lad who cleaned their pool, her tennis coach, the barman from their club, and most humiliating of all, his best friend. That had been the final straw, besides, it was hard to ignore when you walked in and caught them at it in their marital bed. Ethan's cheeks still burned with humiliation when he thought of it. He couldn't believe he'd been so blind, a man who was an expert at reading his patients had missed every clue when it came to his home life. He pulled up in front of his house and let himself in. The hall was dark and unwelcoming, and his unpleasant trip down memory lane earlier had reminded him how empty his house for one was. No one was there to greet him or ask him if he had a good day. He'd considered getting a pet but with his hours he wasn't sure it was fair. Maybe a cat, he mused, they aren't so bothered if you're out all day.

Ethan clicked on a couple of lamps hoping that the soft lighting would make the house look better. Instead, it just cast shadows across the stacks of unpacked boxes reminding him that he hadn't made any effort to settle in. The house itself had the potential to be a lovely home, it just needed some time and attention.

He realised that one of the reasons he'd been thinking about Andrea was because Carrie made him feel the same way she had. He constantly had that edgy impression that she was playing with him and pulling the wool over his eyes. It wasn't anything he could've put his finger on or prove, it was just an instinctive thing that he couldn't shake off.

Was that the problem? Was this case going to be too emotive for him to look at it rationally? Ethan shook his head at himself, how ridiculous, he was just being maudlin. Most of this was probably caused by everyone else's views rather than him forming his own as he usually did. It might take a few sessions, but he was pretty sure he'd get to the bottom of whatever game she was playing. It was probably tied to her denial, never admitting or accepting what she'd done and this was her way of avoiding having to face it. He planned to take her on a journey through her childhood, teenage years, and then up to the murder hoping to get her comfortable enough to open up. Once she had he'd be able to better read her reactions and answers and that would lead to him coming to a conclusion about her risk for his report.

Having settled that in his mind he felt a lot better. Pouring himself a drink he flopped onto the sofa and picked up the book from the side table. He'd read a few chapters and then head up to bed.

Chapter Five

Ethan hadn't even made it as far as a few steps towards his office before one of the staff collared him.

"There was an incident last night with Carrie Martin Doc. Could you come to the wing so we can fill you in?"

Rachel looked eager for him to do that straight away so he nodded and followed her through the corridor to the staff office. There was no sign of any of the inmates this morning and the sound of cutlery clattering and the faint aroma of eggs suggested this was because they were busy eating breakfast. His stomach rumbled despite the smell not being especially appetizing and he thought longingly of how he'd planned to pop to the staff canteen and try out their bacon sandwiches this morning. Gratefully accepting the coffee he was offered he sat down in one of the spare chairs and waited to hear what his newest, and most interesting, patient had been up to.

"After clearing away the evening meal last night we did our usual cutlery count and found one of the knives missing. This triggered a room search and it wasn't long before it was found in Carrie Martin's possession. She'd hidden it by using some tape to stick it under her bed. We confiscated it immediately and put her on watch as per procedure, but no matter who asks her she refuses to tell us what she wanted it for. There's no history of self-harm but we can't rule it out, it's either that or she planned to hurt someone else. We were hoping you'd speak to her and see if you can get it out of her."

Ethan nodded, "I can try but I can't promise I'll do any better than you have. I've barely scratched the surface of who Carrie really is and I can't say she entirely trusts me yet."

The staff exchanged a look before Rachel spoke up.

"It's likely you never will get below the surface with Carrie, we've all tried, but she's a closed book. She'll lie as easily as she breathes and she'll put on whatever personality she thinks will get her what she wants. She's quite possibly the most manipulative, cold prisoner that we've ever had on the wing."

Ethan tried not to frown but he was tired of hearing this same description from everyone involved in her case. He'd seen it before, a particular patient would be challenging and all of the staff would start to view him or her negatively. Even staff who'd never met the patient before would already have preconceived ideas about them and as a result, wouldn't be able to form a positive relationship.

"Okay, bring her along to one of the one-to-one rooms and I'll see what I can find out."

Carrie trembled so hard as the guards led her into the room he could see her visibly shaking. Her pale face and wide eyes full of tears told him how afraid she was as she sat in her seat opposite him. As soon as the guards had left the room she burst into tears and laid her head in her arms sobbing loudly. The thought that she was putting it on to try and avoid being in trouble popped unbidden into his head and he pushed it away. That was the problem with hearing negative things about a person, your gut instinct was to take that into account instead of having an open mind.

He didn't comment, he just waited until she started to calm down. Wiping her eyes with her sleeve she took a deep, shuddering breath.

"So, do you want to tell me what happened last night Carrie? The staff are concerned that you intended to harm yourself."

Carrie dropped her eyes to the table as though ashamed to answer him and when she did it was in a small quiet voice that he had to strain to hear.

"I'm scared Doctor, I'm so frightened I don't even want to tell you what's going on. No one will believe me anyway."

Ethan gave her what he hoped looked like a reassuring smile.

"You'll be safer if you tell me what's going on as I'll be able to help you. I can't help if I don't know can I?"

Carrie nodded slowly, her eyes darted around the room until eventually, they settled on him.

"It's Olive Long, one of the other prisoners. She's got it in for me, she really hates me."

She paused as though not wanting to say anything more.

"Why do you think she hates you?"

Carrie picked at a scratch on the table with her blunt nails, "She whispers in my ear Doctor. She does it all the time when the staff aren't looking, she hisses "Child Catcher." Then she tells me that the punishment for child killers and perverts is, a mug of boiling water and sugar in the face. At dinner, she kept catching my eye and waving her mug at me and I knew she was planning to come for me. I know I shouldn't have done it, but I just hoped if I had a knife to wave at her it might put her off."

Ethan watched her for a moment trying to read her expression and her body language. To him, she looked genuinely afraid, and if what she was telling him was true then he wasn't surprised. Who'd want a mug of boiling water and sugar thrown in their face?

"Thank you for trusting me with that information Carrie. Can you tell me why you didn't feel able to tell the staff what was going on?"

Carrie looked uncomfortable, "I know I should've done but Olive is one of their favourites and I know they don't like me very much. I didn't think they'd listen and if Olive found out I'd grassed she'd come after me for that too."

There was something about what she said that rang true. He knew that the staff weren't exactly sympathetic towards Carrie and he wouldn't be surprised if she'd picked up on it. As if they knew it was a good moment the two guards came back into the room, one of them was Bee Croft. Her sour face bought to mind the phrase, "She looks like she's licking piss off a thistle."

"Get up Martins – time to go back to your cell. You're on close watch thanks to that little stunt you pulled last night."

Ethan winced, it wasn't the most helpful end to his session with Carrie. The frightened look had come back and she threw him an imploring look. It wasn't as though there was anything he could do though, this was prison protocol and he had to step back and let them handle it as they saw fit. Carrie's head dropped as though she was exhausted and she pulled herself clumsily to her feet before shuffling away behind them. Ethan followed them back to the wing, the guards marching Carrie back to her room while he went straight to the office.

Rachel looked surprised to see him back so soon, "Surely you didn't manage to wingle it out of her already?"

Ethan shrugged, "I can only tell you what she told me and it'll be your choice if you believe her or what you do with it."

The prison officer nodded, "Okay, that sounds intriguing."

"She told me that another prisoner called Olive Long has been making some serious threats to hurt her and she stole the knife for self-protection."

Rachel gave him an incredulous look, "I can't see that being true, but in the interests of having the whole story did she say what threats Olive made and why she didn't just report it to us?"

"She said Olive was threatening to throw boiling water and sugar in her face and that she kept whispering "Child Catcher" in her ear when she knew the staff weren't watching. According to Carrie, Olive is a favourite among the staff while she isn't liked, and no one would've believed her."

Rachel rolled her eyes, "Sorry Doc, but what a load of codswallop. Olive isn't capable of making those sorts of threats let alone carrying them out. She's the least scary prisoner on the wing. She's here on Robin because she's vulnerable, she's got a mild learning disability you see."

Ethan considered this additional information, "Does that genuinely make her incapable of threatening anyone though?"

Rachel shook her head, "Doc, I'm going to take you to the quiet room to meet her and you can make your own mind up."

Olive was sitting in one of the armchairs with a pair of headphones covering her ears. With her small face and little legs, she looked like a child as she swung her legs in time with whatever she was listening to. Rachel waved to her and Olive pulled down the headphones.

"Olive, this is Doctor Quinn, he needs to ask you a few questions, is that okay?"

Olive nodded eagerly and turned to Ethan with an inquisitive expression. He crouched down so he was in her eyeline.

"Olive, have you said anything to Carrie Martin that might have made her think you'd hurt her?"

Olive shook her head vigorously.

"Olive, I need to hear you say it out loud please."

The small woman looked anxiously at Rachel before squeaking "No" in a voice that sounded as childlike as she looked.

"Thank you, Olive."

When they got back to the office Rachel cast him a look that seemed a little smug.

"So Doc, do you still feel as though Olive would've been whispering threats in Carrie's ear?"

Ethan shrugged, "I didn't say I believed everything that Carrie told me, I'm well aware of her history, but I did have a responsibility to tell you."

Rachel sighed, "I know you feel that we're overly judgemental about Carrie Martins but we've got good reason to be. Look up her incident reports, especially those from before she was moved to the vulnerable wing."

It had been on Ethan's list of tasks but he hadn't got around to it yet. In fact, he'd been planning to read it with his bacon sandwich this morning. Waving goodbye to the staff he headed straight down to the canteen where he treated himself to a mug of coffee and a large bacon roll that he took upstairs to his office. Before switching on his computer he pulled his notebook over and made a list of the things that Carrie had told him already. He then catagorised them as known lies, potential lies, and possible truths. It made for interesting reading and he wondered what the best way was to address it with Carrie. Should he confront her head-on with the lies about Olive and then challenge some of the other information he wasn't sure about?

Thinking about it he decided that wasn't going to be an effective approach. The best thing was to let her keep talking and then try to work out what was true and what wasn't as they went along. If he went in too hard it might have the effect of creating a barrier that would make her less likely to engage with him. Pushing her file aside he made an effort to focus on some of his other caseload and get through the huge number of new emails he'd had sent to his inbox overnight.

Chapter Six

I t wasn't until after lunch that Ethan finally got around to reading Carrie's old incident reports. Seeing how long the list was he decided to start with the ones that looked serious and then end on the one that had finally led to her being transferred to Robin Wing.

Most of them were incidents where other prisoners were the main players, but Carrie got a mention as being on the sidelines of events. The staff regularly mentioned that she'd been seen near the perpetrator in the lead-up to things kicking off. They suspected she was whispering in their ears and inciting prisoners to fight with each other over perceived slights. To Ethan, this painted a picture of someone who entertained themselves at the expense of others. The final incident in general population was Carrie's riskiest yet. She must've gambled on being moved because if she hadn't been chances were she'd have been badly beaten or even killed over it.

It had all started with a rumour, that Frankie Smith had a mobile phone stashed in her cell but was too selfish to let anyone else use it. Frankie kept denying having one, but the more she denied it, the more the other women felt she was lying to avoid sharing. No one seemed to know where the gossip had originated, but it spread like wildfire among the women. With so much bad feeling it became the talk of the wing and inevitably it didn't take long before the prison officers became aware too. The governor was surprised. Frankie had been an unsettled and challenging prisoner to start with, but once she stopped trying to buck the system she'd settled down nicely in the last twelve months. As a result of her improved behaviour social services had recently agreed to start contact visits with Frankie's four-year-old son. Frankie was very aware that any incident could jeopardise that arrangement. At the weekly update meeting, it was decided that in order to quash or prove the gossip the staff should arrange a cell search. If no phone was found it would end the rumblings of an argument among the women, and if it was..Well, Frankie would be dealt with.

On the day they turned her cell over she seemed unconcerned and the POs saw this as a sign that there'd be nothing to find. They started the search half-heartedly, poking through the cupboards, checking in all the tea and coffee containers, and eventually lifting Frankie's mattress to look underneath. And there it was, in the most common hiding place. Either Frankie was overconfident about not getting found out or she was stupid. Both POs had noted Frankie's stunned look as they pulled it out and put it down to her shock at getting caught. She denied it, of course, pointing the finger at her cellmate, Carrie. Claims of being set up were commonplace and the officers would've brushed her accusations aside had it not been for one of them saying they saw a fleeting smug smile on Carrie's face. Knowing that she'd lost her precious contact with her son Frankie had nothing more to lose. She'd flown at Carrie and managed to get in one good punch to her face before being taken to the ground. Sticking Frankie in solitary while they decided what to do with their problem child it was eventually solved when a bed became available on Robin Wing. Set up to provide a safe environment for prisoners at risk of exploitation or harm it housed a combination of those with mental health, learning disabilities, and those whose crimes against children put them at risk of harm.

Ethan had made himself a few notes while he was reading and was getting a picture of a woman who was capable of taking great risks to get what she wanted. Carrie had requested a transfer to Robin Wing soon after her conviction but she'd been denied. Were all of the incidents on the general population wing created to get her own way? The other view could be that the officers had felt as negatively about Carrie as the staff on Robin and saw her as a perpetrator even when she wasn't. It would be a brave move to risk incurring the wrath of another prisoner like Carrie would've if she had been involved in the phone incident.

It also added another layer to the woman that Ethan was slowly trying to get to know. It was too soon to confront her with his thoughts, but he was keeping a log so he'd be able to slowly trickle his ideas into their conversations. Talking of which it was time to meet with the lady herself.

This time she was already in the room when he arrived, sitting opposite her he smiled.

"You're looking less stressed than last time we met, are things better on the wing now?"

Carrie gave him an enigmatic smile, "It's much the same as it's always been, but I have a feeling it's going to start improving soon."

Ethan was curious about that comment, did she mean that she was going to be making some changes to improve her relationships with others or was she referring to the possibility of parole?

Before he could clarify she leaned forward eagerly, "Would you like me to move on with my history now?"

He nodded, "Yes, I think that's a good place to start. But before we do I would like to clarify what we're doing here. I'm meeting with you to compile a report for your parole hearing, the outcome isn't a given and I'm keeping an open mind. I just want to make sure you're aware that this might not end the way you hope."

Carrie's smile dropped and she lowered her eyes as though hiding tears.

"I do understand Doctor Quinn, and I'm doing my best to engage with you. I'm being open and honest, and all the things that I know you all look for. I am hopeful that I can get out, but I know it probably won't happen so I'm prepared for the worst."

When she raised her head her eyes were bone dry and clear, and Ethan couldn't shake the feeling she was playing with him. Deciding the best option wasn't to feed into it he moved on with the session.

"Tell me about your move into secondary school, did things change for you at that point?"

Carrie nodded, she looked eager to get back into her life story so he got comfortable and let her begin.

Chapter Seven

Carrie

I walked into the secondary school on my first day full of trepidation for what lay ahead. My uniform was brand new and felt stiff and uncomfortable. My dad had managed to get me into a school out of the usual catchment area so no one from my old school was moving up with me. I couldn't help but wonder if that was an opportunity to reinvent myself. Maybe I could be the extrovert that I hadn't been before.

Everything was strange and overwhelming. I clearly remember how it felt to sit in my new form room surrounded by strangers who all seemed to know each other. The strangeness didn't last though, and eventually, some of the girls started to invite me to have lunch at their table in the canteen. At first, I thought I'd be as tongue-tied as I'd been at middle school, but somehow the right words just came to me. From then on it just seemed to work out. I was suddenly the funny one, the rebellious one who'd take a dare and get into fights. I loved it, but unfortunately, it also meant I was getting in a lot of trouble.

My father was very unhappy the first time I came home with a report card for him to sign and my school reports didn't exactly fill him with pride. He tried grounding me, shouting at me, and even deep and meaningful chats, but nothing worked. I was hooked on being popular at long last and I wasn't about to change. It wasn't just my behaviour that was different either, I'd finally blossomed and the ugly duckling became a swan. That meant boys, lots of boys.

I'm ashamed to say I was very promiscuous, I drank, I smoked, and I generally did everything I was told not to do. My school work suffered and before long no matter how bright I couldn't keep the A-grade results my father had been used to. My life was a vicious cycle of sneaking out of the house and getting up to mischief whenever I felt the urge.

My father was already growing increasingly impatient with me, and we'd had a blazing row about his threat to send me away to a girls-only boarding school. You'd think by this time it couldn't get any worse, but I had one last stupid move to make.

Mr Walcott was one of the more popular teachers, tall, well-built, and one of the youngest on the staff team. All the girls had a crush on him. We all flirted like mad despite the poor man making it clear that he wasn't interested in risking his whole career for a fling with a pupil. I was sure I'd seen the light of interest in his eyes though and one afternoon made an excuse to stay back after our lesson. Sashaying over to his desk I made sure to accidentally reveal more leg than I should've before faking a trip and landing conveniently in his lap.

In my imagination, he'd be so overcome by passion that he'd immediately press his lips against mine and I'd have him, just as I'd had every other boy I'd set my cap at. The complete opposite happened, he scooted backward so fast that I fell onto the floor and then he dragged me to the head's office to tell him what I'd done.

The school called my father, who when he heard what I'd done looked so ashamed of me I could've cried. I didn't, I just stared defiantly at the head as she listed the reasons why my behaviour was inappropriate and that she had a good mind to expel me. Despite my attempts to act as though I didn't care, I did realise that I had to pull my socks up. I didn't become a goody two shoes overnight, but I did focus a bit more on my studies and a lot less on mucking about.

I eventually left with a decent set of results and decided that I wanted to pursue a career in teaching. I got all the information together and excitedly told my father who I thought would be pleased I was planning such a steady job for myself. Instead, he laughed in my face and told me that we couldn't afford university and to put that thought out of my head. I was devastated, I'd made no plans beyond that and now had no idea what I was going to do with myself. Sitting around and not working longer term wasn't on the cards either and it didn't take my dad long to start nagging me about finding a job. He'd point out adverts for staff wanted at the local supermarket and I'd feel a little piece of me die each time I thought about it.

Then one day I saw an ad looking for staff to work in the local library, I loved books and reading and thought how ideal it would be. I couldn't believe my luck when I was offered the job and I was happy there for a while.

Chapter Eight

Carrie trailed off and Ethan thought he knew why. They were getting closer to the main event and it was probably playing on her mind how she was going to move forward with her story without disclosing anything she hadn't said before. At that point, it would be almost impossible to weave fact and fiction for him as a lot of it was now a matter of public record. Ethan pointed to the clock and saw a look of relief on her face as he explained their time was up. The POs whisked her away and Ethan headed back to his office to shut everything up so he could go home. It was Friday and that meant two whole days off. He'd been planning to unpack a few more boxes and try and make his home look more like someone lived there. That was before Carrie had crept into his head and taken over, now he was tempted to try and do some detective work.

It wasn't unusual for a doctor to talk to a patient's next of kin to get a full family history, but Ethan had a feeling his boss wouldn't endorse his plan to go and speak to Carrie's father. He thought about it all the way home. His number and address were in her file and he'd copied it down on a Post-it note before leaving the office. It was more a bending than a breaking of the rules, he assured himself as he walked by the security at the front of the building. He wasn't taking a file home, just a little note that he could follow up on over the weekend.

At home, a takeaway on order and a glass of red wine in his hand, Ethan wasn't so certain he should go ahead. If Carrie's father complained to the prison he'd definitely be for it. The scrap of bright yellow paper mocked him from the coffee table and he impulsively picked it up before tapping the numbers into his mobile.

"Hello, is that Stanley Martins?

The voice that replied sounded a little coarse as though rusty through lack of use.

"Yeah, that's me. I don't give interviews so don't bother asking."

Ethan guessed that as the father of one of the country's most notorious child killers, he would get a lot of calls wanting him to sell his story.

"I'm Dr Ethan Quinn and I'm currently doing a report on your daughter for her parole hearing. I was hoping it would be possible for us to meet up and talk so I can get a proper family history for her."

The pause went on long enough that Ethan thought Stanley was about to hang up on him.

"I guess so. You don't need me to talk about the murders, do you? That I can't do."

"No, just her history, what she was like as a child, and if with hindsight there were any signs that she had problems."

"Okay. I can't do weekdays because I work, the only time I can manage is weekends. I'm home tomorrow all day, I'm not going anywhere so just come when you're ready."

Ethan gave a sigh of relief, he'd been wondering how to approach the idea of meeting up at a weekend and the answer had fallen in his lap. Quickly agreeing he made a note of the directions before Mr

Martins abruptly hung up on him. Well, he was committed now, no backing out.

Mr Martins shuffled to the front door in his tartan slippers. He looked like a mad professor with his wild white hair, bushy eyebrows, and long hooked nose. He waved Ethan in and led the way to the kitchen at the back of the house. The room had seen better days, the lino on the floor was curling up in places and the sink was full of dirty dishes.

"Would you like a drink, Dr Quinn?"

Ethan nodded, "Only if you're having one Mr Martins, don't put yourself to any bother."

"Call me Stan."

The blunt words were tossed over his shoulder as he filled the kettle and got two mugs out of the cupboard. Dumping a tea bag in each and adding a splash of milk and two sugars he was clearly making Ethan's drink to match his own tastes. Ethan, who preferred coffee and didn't take sugar, thought it was better to just accept what he was offered.

"Please call me Ethan, Dr. Quinn sounds very formal."

Slapping the mugs down on the table Stan took a seat at the opposite side.

"Well, whatcha want to know? I must've gone over this a thousand times, do none of you people ever take notes?"

Ethan smiled disarmingly, "It's always better to hear it from someone personally. If you could just talk me through her early years up to adult that would be really helpful."

Stan rubbed his hands together as though cold despite the stuffiness of the room.

"There weren't much trouble with her as a baby, she was an easy one, slept through from early on, and didn't give us any problems. It was hard, what with her mum the way she was, and then when she walked out on us it seemed to trigger a change in the kid. Always grizzling and demanding, I was a single dad with two nippers to raise, what was I supposed to do?"

Ethan blinked a few times but didn't speak. What on earth? This was nothing like Carrie's version at all. A mum who walked out? Two nippers? So there was a sibling then?

Stan didn't seem to notice Ethan's confusion as he carried on with his history lesson.

"Carrie was just seven when she left and her little brother, Dan, was only two. There was me, a working man with a toddler and a seven-year-old to juggle on my own. My Mandy did fuck all, mostly she was too drunk to give a shit, but at least she was here in the day for the kids while I was working."

Ethan was scribbling down notes as fast as he could, this was all stuff that he planned to use for his first mild challenges of the discrepancies in Carrie's version of events.

"Carrie changed almost overnight. She became clingy, didn't want to go to school, crying all the time. The teachers said she was struggling at school with her reading, and it just got worse after Mandy left. In hindsight, I wish I'd got some help for her, but it wasn't the way I was raised. You were supposed to cope with your own problems not go running to some do-gooder. It got even worse at secondary school, she fell right behind, but at least she was trying harder. She didn't have many friends and I did feel sorry that she was so lonely. Then there was that weird shit with her teacher. Threw herself at him, sitting on his lap and trying it on, unbuttoning her shirt in front of him. I was so ashamed I wished the ground would open up and swallow me."

Another note, this time that Carrie appeared to have added a little layer of truth to the story she'd told him.

"You said about that hindsight thing. Well, looking back she did seem to live in a weird fantasy world. I never knew if she was telling me the truth or not, she'd look me dead in the eye as she told the biggest whoppers. People were always accusing her of shit. Saying she'd played stupid pranks and whatnot, I'd ask her about it and I never knew if she was lying or not."

He looked distant, as though reliving it before slurping down his now lukewarm tea. Ethan took a sip and managed not to grimace at the cold, overly sweet, and strangely greasy taste.

"Then she did her exams. Did better than we'd thought she would, but not good enough for university which I'd always hoped for. I tried to get her to go to college, maybe retake some of them and get better outcomes the next time but she wasn't interested. "I've had enough of school Daddy." So, next thing I knew she'd got herself a job in the town library and I thought she was all settled. Decent job, meet a nice guy, settle down, and give me a few grand kiddies."

Stan sighed, "Instead she did something so terrible that even I can't forgive her."

• • • ● ● ● ● ● • •

Ethan sat in his car outside Stan's house and read through the notes he'd made. Carrie was clearly weaving some truth into the stories she was telling him. There was the teacher for example and the job at the library, but a lot of it simply wasn't true. He could put some of it down to reinventing an ordinary, if lonely, childhood, but the big ones like specifically describing herself as an only child were strange lies to tell. Why would she disregard her younger brother so completely? It was understandable to some extent that the alcoholic mother who walked out became a more sympathetic figure. To get to the bottom of it he'd need to dig deeper, and that's where he was now feeling uncertain. It was one thing to speak to a close family member who was logged as next of kin, but it was far more murky ethically to seek out anyone else.

If he could he'd like to hear from someone from both schools, and her brother might have some interesting insights. Siblings often had a different take on the family dynamics than the parents. Ethan sighed, for now, he was going to have to go home and try to put the enigma that was Carrie out of his head.

Chapter Nine

Ethan slept late on Sunday, and by the time he got up the sun was at full height and it was gone 10 am. It was his favourite day, one where he had nothing planned and it stretched ahead of him full of endless relaxation. He started with a mug of bean-to-cup coffee and then made himself a poached egg on toast which he ate while reading his book. Ethan pushed all thoughts of work, and particularly Carrie, out of his head. He planned to have a day without thinking about her as he put on the radio to drown out his thoughts. A quick shower and he was soon lounging around the house in his comfortable track pants and a baggy shirt. Ethan's eye fell on the stack of boxes, he should really make a start on unpacking. Unable to face it he decided to leave it until later, although he was pretty sure he'd find another excuse by then. He was just about to pick up his book when his mobile rang, and a quick glance at the screen made him answer quickly. Part of his new role meant sharing the on-call rota with the other senior clinicians and this was his first weekend.

It was Rachel from Robin Wing, and she sounded stressed.

"It's Olive, she's hurt herself badly and we need you here. Ambulance is on its way but we believe this has something to do with Carrie."

Not wanting to get into it over the phone Ethan promised he'd be straight over and hastily hung up. After a quick change of clothes, smart casual as it was a Sunday, he raced out to his car. On the short journey to the prison, he went over the sparse details from the call. Until he got there he wouldn't know exactly why the staff thought Carrie was involved, or how Olive had harmed herself or how badly.

Once there he jogged to the main reception and rushed through the security checks to get to the wing. Rachel was hovering by the office door clearly waiting for him to arrive. Weekend staffing was notoriously minimal and apart from Rachel, Ethan didn't recognise any of the other staff on site. Agency staff often made up the numbers on the more unsociable shifts which wasn't ideal, but that was the only way to keep close to safe levels of staffing.

"The ambulance has just left with Olive and the cleaning crew is in her room getting rid of the blood. It was horrible, so horrible..."

She tailed off and Ethan left a therapeutic silence between them while she put together what she wanted to say next.

"One of the agency staff told me they could hear strange noises from Olive's room. Of course, they didn't bother checking on her and just came to fetch me which meant a delay in getting to her. I've never seen her like that before. She was running the full length of her room and smashing her head into the wall over and over. There was blood everywhere, all over the walls, and floors, and pouring down Olive's face. It was like a mask of blood."

Rachel shuddered, "It took me and two of the agency guys to hold her still, and even then she was fighting to get free and carry on. That's when I spotted Carrie peering around the door watching with that nasty little smile of hers. I told her to get the hell away from the incident and she just shrugged at me and walked off. Then Steve, one of the better agency staff we get, told me he'd seen Carrie hanging around Olive all day talking to her really quietly so he couldn't hear what she was saying."

Her face darkened, "Imagine picking on someone as vulnerable as Olive, that woman's a monster."

Ethan, who tried to avoid emotively negative terms like that, just nodded reassuringly. Rachel was too upset right now for him to challenge her on her assumption, but he also wasn't going to join in with blaming the "unpopular prisoner."

"I'll speak to Carrie, try and find out what her take on it is. Maybe with the incident being so fresh she'll let something slip, but don't pin your hopes on it. So far I've found her to be very careful about what she shares with me."

It was a subdued Carrie that was led into the 1:1 room. Her hair was a tangled mess that she pushed back impatiently and her shirt stained with what looked like the remnants of breakfast. Ethan had never seen her disheveled before.

"Is Olive okay? Please tell me you haven't bought me in here to tell me she's dead?"

Ethan shook his head, "I haven't had an update on Olive's condition as yet. I wanted to have a chat because the staff are reporting you were spending a lot of time with Olive before the incident."

Carrie's mouth dropped open and she flinched as though physically trying to remove herself from the conversation.

"Surely the staff don't think I had anything to do with this? Do they think I'm some sort of monster?"

Almost exactly what Rachel had said, he thought.

"I was called in because of the mental health implications and I wondered if Olive said anything to you that in hindsight could explain why she suddenly self-harmed."

Ethan took note of the swift momentary flash of triumph on Carrie's face. It was gone so quickly he wondered if he'd imagined it as she wiped her eyes with the cuff of her ragged cardigan.

"She was just her usual self Dr Quinn, talking about how much she misses her mum and complaining that she didn't like the eggs at breakfast. She did keep saying sorry to me for the things she'd said about hurting me."

Carrie gave a shocked expression as though something had just occurred to her.

"You don't think she felt that bad about threatening me, do you? I kept telling her it was okay and not to worry, maybe I should've told one of the staff. It's just that they so obviously hate me I don't feel comfortable going to them."

Ethan couldn't read anything more than genuine concern in her face but he couldn't shake the gut feeling that this was a convenient way to raise that she'd been telling the truth about Olive's threats. Considering that he was already building a picture of how she wove stories filled with untruths, half-truths, and the full truth, it was hard to unpick if what she was saying now was exactly that. If it was, which parts were true? There was always a thread of the truth running through each story. Was this her way of telling him that she'd manipulated Olive as a punishment for calling her "Child Catcher?" Then another idea occurred to him, had she done this to make sure her story was believed? What better way to convince everyone than for Olive to be so full of remorse that she tried to kill herself?

He tried not to outwardly show any signs of the disgust that was burning his stomach like acid but he was sure he saw Carrie flick her gaze more intensely on his face. He had two options right now, either confront her with some of her lies and see how she responded or hold off until he had more to go on. Weighing it up, he thought how easily Carrie could just call her dad the liar and that would leave him with a he said/she said scenario. No, best to wait until he could put things together better and she didn't have as much wriggle room.

Carrie looked almost disappointed as he thanked her for trying to help, but she hid it well under her mask of innocence. Ethan had a stern word with himself as she was led back to the wing. He needed to retain his impartiality otherwise he was at risk of making potentially unfair observations based on circumstantial evidence and other people's opinions. Going back to his office he downloaded the session onto his computer with the others and left himself a note to remember to watch them back next week.

Outside the prison, he was about to climb in his car when a bright flash drew his attention to the prison gate. A man was standing on the other side and the flash had been caused by the sun's glare off the screen of his phone that he was holding aloft in Ethan's direction.

Something about the man gave Ethan a bad feeling, which grew as the man turned and fast walked away as Ethan approached him. Without thinking it through he followed him, speeding up his own pace to try and narrow the gap between them. Finally, the man stopped and breathing heavily leaned on a nearby wall.

"Why are you photographing me?"

Ethan stayed a safe distance from the man in case he turned out to be dangerous, but with him struggling to catch his breath he had to admit he didn't seem up to the task of assaulting anyone.

"I'm a journalist."

The man was still panting as he bent forward and put his hands on his knees for a moment. That seemed to have done the trick because he was more able to speak when he lifted his head again.

"Callum Winters, but everyone calls me Cal."

The man handed Ethan a business card.

"I'm a freelancer and I'm hoping to write an article on Carrie Martin's parole outcome, maybe even a book if I get enough information. I'm going to be speaking to her family and people who knew her back then. You're that new doctor for the prison so I'm guessing you've met her."

Cal looked eager for details and Ethan shook his head.

"No go I'm afraid, that pesky old confidentiality applies here."

The journalist shrugged, "Always worth a try Doc. Anyway, keep my card, and if you ever feel differently give me a ring."

Ethan watched him walk away thoughtfully. On the one hand, Cal would be the perfect way to find out what he needed to know about Carrie. On the other, it wouldn't be all give and no take, he'd be expecting Ethan to chip in information of his own and there was no way he could do that.

Chapter Ten

M onday morning had come around in the blink of an eye. After tossing and turning for much of the night he'd finally fallen asleep in the early hours until rudely awakened by his alarm. Ethan treated himself to a coffee from the staff canteen on his way upstairs and hadn't long settled himself in front of his emails when there was a knock at the door.

May poked her head around and he waved her in, she looked tense and the reason soon became clear.

"There's no easy way to say this so I'll just come out with it. Olive passed away a few hours ago from her injuries. I've just been over to the wing to see how everyone's holding up and the staff are definitely not in a good place. They feel as though it's Carrie's fault and knowing there's nothing that can be done to prove it is causing a lot of frustration. I'd suggest you take her off for a long chat away from them to ease the tensions."

Ethan felt a wave of sadness for poor Olive, he'd looked into her case and she was here after lashing out at a child who'd been picking on her for months. She wasn't known to be violent, and if it hadn't been a child she'd hit she probably wouldn't have got this custodial sentence. He couldn't blame the staff for feeling the way they did. He had his own misgivings about Carrie, but May was right, there was definitely a need for an intervention.

Rachel was on shift again, her face rigid and angry as she told him about Olive and vented some of her feelings.

"I can't help it, I just feel sick every time I look at her. She can deny it until she's blue in the face, but I know she said something that set Olive off."

Ethan nodded, "I was thinking I'd arrange a longer-than-usual session with her. Get her out from under your feet while everyone processes what happened."

"Thanks, Doc, I appreciate it. Maybe you could use the gardens for a change? It's a nice day and there's a shaded area to sit in. I'll ask Croft to take you out."

The thought of being outside had been a welcome idea that was suddenly less appealing now he had to endure the company of the sour-faced Bee Croft. The woman herself wasn't any more pleased than he was when she appeared with Carrie in tow.

"This is outside the usual arrangements Rachel, I don't like it. Why should this one get special dispensation?"

She jerked her chin at Carrie who stood stoically in place not showing any reaction. Rachel shrugged and didn't bother replying as Bee huffed and strode off in the direction of the exit to the outside areas.

Garden might not have been the description that sprung to mind for most people when they saw it. When Rachel had described a seat in the shade he'd conjured up sitting under a tree with the grass under his feet. Instead, it was a sparse concrete area with a narrow rim of wilting, brown grass around the outside of it. The shaded seating area was a wooden bench table that had seen better days covered by an overhanging structure that may once have been a pergola.

Croft settled herself on a bench just out of hearing range as they took the table. He watched her dig in her pockets and pull out her cigarettes before lighting up. Carrie saw where he was looking and gave a chuckle.

"The irony of a woman who kicks off that this isn't protocol and then breaks the no smoking on duty rule."

Ethan didn't feel it was appropriate to agree with her so said nothing before turning the conversation to Olive.

"Has someone told you the news about Olive?"

Carrie nodded, "Terrible news. Poor Olive, I do hope she's at peace now."

The words were right but her tone was just that little bit off, as though she'd planned what to say in advance. She must've realised that she wasn't hitting the right note because she suddenly threw her head into her arms and started sobbing.

"I get blamed for everything. It's always my fault. I got moved here because I was wrongly accused of setting up my cellmate. It's been the same my whole life."

She lifted her head, her eyes looked red and swollen but he couldn't shake the feeling that there was something coldly calculating about her behaviour. Ethan dug deep and pulled up his objectivity, it was easy to fall into a trap of looking for reactions and then assuming what they meant. When you had almost the whole staff team telling you negative things it was hard to put them aside. Carrie had already told him enough about her childhood for him to recognise the potential that she'd suffered some emotional neglect. This sort of history would often lead someone to finding it hard to hit the right emotional notes and could make them appear cold and unfeeling. In a bid to meet social expectations people with Carrie's background often overreacted, and this could be the case here.

"What do you mean by everyone Carrie? From our previous conversations, it seemed like your childhood was pretty okay."

Ethan played it down in the hopes that this would prompt a bit more honesty. A tactic that appeared to have worked.

Carrie blushed, "I may have been a little economical with the truth. I find it hard to trust people so I've made up my own history, and I've got so used to telling it that I find it hard to talk about the real one."

Ethan mentally noted how she'd used a careful euphemism for lying "economical with the truth." He didn't comment though and encouraged her to continue.

"I think it would help if you told me the real story, Carrie. I'm here to help you and I can't do that unless I know everything."

Chapter Eleven
Carrie

The truth is that my father was physically violent towards me. Not just physically either, he emotionally abused me too. He was cold, unfeeling, and cruel. It was bad enough as a child when he'd slap my legs, or spank me, and then send me to bed without dinner. I cried myself to sleep, hungry and sore and wishing someone loved me. I don't remember much of my mum, but I like to think she was his opposite and that she at least loved me.

By the time I started secondary school, he'd got even worse. As I developed into a woman he started to get paranoid about boys and me getting pregnant and bringing shame on him. He'd say things like "I smell the alcohol on your breath you dirty whore." "I know the boys are touching you, you dirty slut."

I just threw myself into staying out of his way as much as I could. I'd stay with friends as often as possible and avoid going home. Mostly I broke the rules at school just to get detention because it was better than going home to him. At home, he treated me like a house servant. I cooked all of our meals, cleaned, did the washing, and waited on him hand and foot when he came in from work.

I'd catch him looking at me sometimes, he'd have this glow in his eyes as though he was weighing me up. He made me uncomfortable. It reminded me of the way the boys at school were starting to look at me and I knew it wasn't right. I went out more and more and came home later and later. It was worth the punishment just to be away from him.

It all came to a head with the incident with that teacher. It was another lie I told you I'm afraid, he was the one who touched me and when another member of staff came into the room he claimed I'd thrown myself at him. I was too scared to tell the truth, I knew my father wouldn't believe me and I'd get twice the punishment for lying.

That night he beat me so badly I couldn't go to school the next day, he told them I was too ashamed and he was letting me stay home to think about my bad behaviour. The school liked that, it sounded as though I was accepting being in the wrong, so no one questioned it. He had to give me a note for games for nearly a month so I didn't change in front of anyone who might see the marks he left on me.

I think he frightened himself with that outburst because he didn't touch me again. That didn't stop him from deriding me, mocking me, and making me give up my dreams, but at least he stopped hitting me. The day I started working was the day I started saving up my money to get out of there. Every time he was cruel or unkind I would check my savings account and see how close I was to my target of getting away from him. I wanted out of his house and out of that town. I had nothing to keep me there.

Chapter Twelve

Carrie stopped abruptly and Ethan was sure it was the thought that her plans to escape were ended the day she'd gone into the woods with three children who'd never come out again. Again, she'd left her brother out of the story, did he have an equally bad time at home as her, or was he the favoured, child?

There'd also been a hint of something sexually inappropriate in this new version of her childhood. She hadn't elaborated, but maybe that was something she might address later on when they'd built a stronger relationship. It made him wonder if the real monster was her father. Was Stan Martins responsible for shaping the woman who'd killed those children?

"You mentioned being blamed for everything, was that just your father?"

She shook her head, "I don't know why, but whenever something happened everyone looked at me. School and home, it was never any different. Maybe I just have one of those faces that everyone likes to blame."

Carrie looked exhausted as though the retelling had been almost as hard as living through it. They'd been out here for over an hour and a half and he could see that Bee was staring in their direction. When she saw they weren't talking anymore she stomped over.

"I can't be sitting around here all day. We're understaffed as it is without you monopolising my time like this."

Carrie got shakily to her feet and Bee took a firm grip on her arm. He saw Carrie wince at the pressure applied and he shot the officer a hard glare. She caught it and returned it, but she did loosen her grip. He followed them back inside where Carrie was given little choice but to go to her room. It was clear that the staff were still feeling sore and weren't keen to have to look at her today. Carrie gave Ethan one final look as she went through her door, it was part sadness, but also partly full of curiosity. Ethan felt as though she was trying to read him and intentionally kept his face expressionless.

The day flew by after that. Ethan had other prisoners to see and he did his best to push Carrie out of his head and focus on them as much as they deserved. Most of the people he was seeing veered from one end of the spectrum to the other. There were the floridly unwell with psychotic symptoms, and then those who struggled with coping with prison life leading to incidents of self-harm and threats of suicide. In its own way, it was depressing. Too many of the people he saw clearly couldn't function, and he wondered when therapeutic input would become the norm instead of throwing people into the ill-equipt prison system.

He ended his day with a disheartening conversation with his community counterpart where he attempted to find more appropriate beds for the most unwell on his caseload.

"I'd love to take them all Ethan, but the reality is that I can't. There's so few secure unit beds now that we've got people in the community that pose a real danger to the public and nothing we can do about it. I can squeeze one, maybe two tops of your guys into the system."

Ethan hated this part of his job, handing out the crumbs of dwindling resources and having to decide who got help and who didn't. Better two than none at all, he tried to tell himself as he swept his eyes down his list.

"Terry Hodges and Susan Frank. I'll send their risk assessments and backgrounds over by email."

Ethan hung up and looked at the clock on the wall, it was half an hour past his official finishing time. He tried to focus on the positives, at least he'd got the potential of two transfers, but he felt drained and empty.

On the way home he couldn't get Carrie out of his head, his curiosity was burning bright and he needed to know more about her. His eye landed on the journalist's card and he tried to ignore the voice that told him this was the answer. If he got caught sharing confidential information with a journalist he'd be sacked on the spot.

There was always the halfway option though, what if he explained that he couldn't tell him anything? Offered nothing but took what he could? Maybe he could hint that he'd open the door later and then back out once he got what he wanted.

Pulling up outside his house he plucked up the card, who was he kidding, he'd be calling the guy as soon as he'd got inside.

Cal had been pleased to hear from him, but less so when he realised it was going to be a one-way street.

"Oh come on Doc, how fair is that?"

"That's the only way I can get involved Cal, take it or leave it."

The journalist pondered for a moment but clearly decided that it was worth it. That or he hoped to wheedle something out of Ethan at the first opportunity. Now they were sitting in Mrs. Grant's house. She'd been Carrie's primary school teacher and had only agreed to see them once Cal had told her he was bringing the doctor with him. Her house was neat and practical, she'd sat them down with refreshments and had handed them a school album that contained all her treasured pictures of her ex-pupils. Carrie stared out at them with a serious expression that didn't sit comfortably on her young face.

"That was taken a short while after her mother left. Poor child was devastated, and from what I could see didn't get much support from her father."

She paused and glanced at both men as though unsure if she should continue. Ethan smiled reassuringly.

"It must be so difficult to go back over such long-ago memories, we really appreciate your help."

She sighed before continuing, " I guess my concerns started way back when Carrie first started with us. She was scruffy, her uniform was in need of replacing and she'd often wear it long after she'd out-grown it. Her mother was nearly always late bringing her in and col-lecting her. On one occasion we had to call her father because she was clearly too inebriated to take responsibility for the child. I remember that day so well, her big blue eyes were full of tears and she looked so frightened."

Ethan tried to picture a little Carrie, scared and neglected but found it hard to imagine.

"She could be a difficult child. Understandable considering the circumstances, but her behaviour did make her unpopular with the other children."

"Were there any particular incidents you could share as an example?"

The retired teacher nodded, "It wasn't really any one thing in particular. It was just that Carrie could be rather sly. She'd "accidentally" tattle tale on the other children, or make a comment that would end up causing a fight. I think she was just a bit socially unskilled. I can't say there was any real malice in it. But I did have my concerns about her home life..."

She drifted off and looked uncomfortable, "There was nothing big enough to report, it was just I got the impression that dad could be a bit withdrawn as a parent. He didn't really show up to parent's evenings and he wouldn't let his children go to anyone's house for a playdate."

Ethan leaned in closer, "Did you teach Carrie's brother too?"

Mrs Grant nodded, "Oh yes, lovely little lad, but so quiet. He'd sit in the corner of the playground reading books rather than playing with the other children."

To Ethan that sounded like Carrie's description of herself at that age, had she swapped stories with the little brother she wouldn't even admit existed?

Chapter Thirteen

Carrie was back to the version of herself that oozed confidence. Sitting down opposite Ethan she crossed her legs and gave him a steady look that suggested the shutters were up and she was ready for his questions. He noticed how she stared directly at the camera at one point. Ethan greeted her warmly and made the split-second decision that he should start asking her about the anomalies in her stories.

"I thought we could talk about your brother today Carrie. I don't want to jump to conclusions but it intrigues me why you've always painted yourself as an only child."

He took in the flash of annoyance at being challenged that passed across her face before she replaced it with a sad smile.

"Poor Dan, he was always such a quiet boy, it was often as though we didn't notice him at all. It felt very much as though it was just me and dad so I guess I've got used to describing myself as not having any siblings."

Carrie shrugged, "I haven't seen him since I was sent here so he doesn't feature in my life at all. My father occasionally writes since I started refusing his requests for visiting orders, but I really don't have a family anymore. It's just me."

Was this a narcissistic view of self so common with sociopathy or did she genuinely feel alone? She was so good with the front she put on that Ethan wasn't entirely sure.

"If I was to interview your father to get a history for you, do you think he'd remember things the way you do?"

Carrie narrowed her eyes, "Have you spoken to my father? He's a pathological liar who will say anything to make himself look good, it'd be a waste of your time talking to him."

It was interesting to hear her describe her father in much the same terms as she was described by others. Ethan wasn't dismissing it though, it was just as likely that her father was the source of her own relationship with the truth.

"It might be helpful to hear his version of events though, and maybe your brother's too. Sometimes other people see things that we miss or misread ourselves."

Carrie's face was dark with anger and she wasn't doing anything to hide it now. It felt as though Ethan had just torn off her mask and he could see the rage underneath it.

"I thought you were interested in me! Just me. But no, as always it's about proving I'm the liar you always thought I was. Go on, do what you want, you will anyway. Talk to anyone, dig the dirt, and find the skeletons in my closet. Why should I care? I thought I could trust you, but you're just like the rest of them."

Ethan let her words settle between them while he considered his answer. In a way she'd just made things easier for him, he had her permission to talk to the people he needed to. The problem was that he had to rebuild trust with her.

"Carrie, I can see how angry I've made you. That wasn't my intention, but we do have to examine what you're telling me so my report shows that you're being open and honest."

She shrugged, the anger dialed down a little but still fizzled in the background.

"I told you, talk to anyone you want. Not many will have anything nice to say about me, but I'll leave you to work out what to believe and what to discard."

He took note of how she'd pre-warned him of hearing bad things. Was that because their opinions had been shaped by what she'd done or were there things in her past?

• • • ● ●•● ● • •

A quick call to Cal confirmed that he'd had no joy in finding Carrie's brother.

"I tried Dan and Daniel, and even Danny, but nada. Usually, my sources can find anyone but no joy with this one."

Ethan thanked him, and once he'd hung up turned his mind to the one database that would hold records for Dan Martins. He could access the health system, and it was nigh on impossible that Dan wouldn't have come up at some point over the last fifteen years. Ethan tapped his pen on his desk and considered the risk of getting caught. The problem was, he knew deep down he was going to go for it anyway.

The right Daniel Martins was at the top of his search list. It had to be him, he was the only one with a birth date that made him the right age and he was fairly local. His address was one that Ethan was familiar with – Standhope Secure Hospital.

Now that was a turn-up, and looking at the dates it seemed he'd been in there since a little less than a year after Carrie was arrested. Remembering the description of him being an overly quiet child maybe he'd always been on the cusp and her crime had pushed him over the edge.

The only way to find out was to use his credentials to get in for a visit. Had Carrie known when she'd told him to knock himself out talking to people from her past that they'd struggle to find Dan? Maybe she hoped he'd stay hidden away in that hospital unable to spill any family secrets.

Ethan had played tug of war with his conscience for a short time. Ultimately he was feeling so invested in finding out the truth there was no way he couldn't go and see Dan. The hospital itself was built out in the middle of nowhere. A large, grey, imposing building surrounded by fields and trees it reminded Ethan of the institutions of the past. A place where people spent whole lifetimes being force-fed medication and enduring treatments that made them worse not better. He shuddered, the history of mental health was littered with a lack of care and a lot of stigma.

Once inside Ethan found it was unexpectedly bright and cheerful. Flashing his badge at the receptionist he was greeted with a friendly smile and a promise to fetch someone to help him. He'd barely taken his seat when a casually dressed young woman in her late twenties appeared next to him with her hand out.

"You must be Dr Quinn. I'm Dr Alexander, but please call me Stella."

"And you must call me Ethan. I'm here to ask about Daniel Martins."

Stella nodded, "Tammy on reception said as much. If you don't mind me asking what is your interest in Dan? No one has shown any interest in him for over a decade. Is it to do with his sister?"

"Yes, it is in a way. I'm the clinician responsible for preparing the report for Carrie's parole hearing. While I've been interviewing her she told me she was an only child, and when I found out that wasn't true it got me thinking why she'd lie."

Stella shrugged, "I'm not sure you'll find any answers here, Ethan. Dan was virtually catatonic when he arrived with us. Although that's no longer the case he rarely speaks, and apart from the basics of using the bathroom, drinking, and eating his only other interest is in drawing horrifically dark pictures that he pins all over his walls. Layer after layer of them on top of each other. No one has ever got to the bottom of his psychiatric diagnosis, and he's proved to be treatment-resistant to every medication we've tried him on. All that works is calming him with a benzodiazepine on the occasions he gets agitated."

"Would I be able to see him?"

Stella gave him a sad smile, "I've got no issue with you seeing him Ethan, but don't expect to get much out of him."

She led the way onto the secure ward. The corridors were painted in calming blues and sunny yellows giving a feeling of being at the beach on a nice day. Stella saw him looking around and laughed.

"I know, totally different from what you think it'll look like from the outside, isn't it? We might have been allocated a building that looks like something out of a gothic horror, but at least we can make the inside more therapeutic."

Stella called a greeting to the nurse in the goldfish bowl office, "We're off to Dan's room."

The nurse nodded and made a note as Stella swept him along to one of the rooms halfway down the corridor. She gave a cursory knock before opening the door.

"I'll leave you to it, back in ten minutes. You won't need much longer than that."

The room was dimly lit and it took Ethan's eyes a while to adjust. Once they did he could make out that the room was sparsely furnished with just the basics. Bed, wardrobe, drawers, and a desk with a chair where Dan was currently sat. Coloured pencils were scattered all over the surface, Dan was bent over a sheet of paper scribbling furiously. He didn't even look up as Ethan came in.

"Hi Dan, I'm Dr Quinn. I've been working with your sister, Carrie."

On the surface, it appeared that Dan hadn't reacted to his introduction at all, but Ethan had noticed the slight widening of his eyes and the catching of his breath.

As Stella had said the walls were papered in Dan's artwork. Every picture was a nightmare image in black and red. Stick figures covered in blood with round screaming faces, and black trees with branches that resembled a monster's arms reaching out to a red sky. Ethan removed his mobile phone and took some photographs so he could look more closely later.

It was as he was zooming in that he spotted one that made him catch his breath. One small red shoe was surrounded by puddles of what looked like blood. As Ethan walked closer to it, Dan stopped his frantic drawing and turned his face toward him. He stared at Ethan and for a moment their eyes met. Instead of dullness of thought Dan's eyes held an interest in Ethan that seemed outside of what Stella described as his usual behaviour.

"That's a good picture, Dan, what can you tell me about it?"

Dan's hair was a wild tangle over his pale hollow face, and his mouth opened and closed a few times like a fish seeking air. He shook his head before returning his attention to the new picture he was creating. More screaming faces, eyes just a harsh pencil line while the liberal use of red created an open mouth full of blood.

His eyes slipped toward Ethan briefly as though checking he was still watching before refocusing on the picture.

"That's a first. He barely acknowledges anyone, even staff he's known his whole stay. Yet you, a complete stranger, are deemed worthy of notice."

Stella had come back into the room in time to see the look Dan had flashed Ethan's way. He noticed Dan didn't so much as pause in his drawing but his shoulders tensed slightly as though annoyed by the intrusion.

"I'd imagine you were just curious about the stranger in your room, hey Dan?"

Ethan addressed his answer to the man furiously drawing, it didn't sit right with him to talk about a patient as though they weren't there.

Stella nodded, "I expect that's it. If you're all done it's time for the medication rounds."

As Ethan followed her out of the door he took in the grotesque wallpaper one last time. What was inside Dan's head that was creating these horrific images?

Chapter 14
Chapter Fourteen

C al had got to the pub ahead of him, his pint of ale only held a few inches of liquid. Waving to Ethan he then gestured toward his drink.

"Didn't know what you drank so I wasn't sure what to get you."

Ethan hid a smile as Cal called to him on his way to the bar.

"Mine's a speckled hen."

The man was growing on him. He was a typical journalist, annoying with his persistent questioning and digging, but he was also witty, intelligent, and genuinely interested in this story. When Ethan returned with two pints Cal took a long gulp before launching into what he'd been up to. Ethan was glad he did because he still wasn't sure how much he should share. It didn't feel right to tell him about Dan. If it got into the papers it wouldn't take much to find out he was the source. Besides that, Dan was entitled to his privacy, if it became common knowledge where he was the hospital would be besieged by the press wanting to catch a snap of him or get a quote from one of the staff.

"I've started on Carrie's secondary school, it's amazing how easy it is to get people gossiping in a small town. One of the biggest scandals, apart from her of course, had to do with one of the male teachers. I don't know how it plays into Carrie's story if it does at all. Apparently, this guy was caught being inappropriate with a female pupil. The woman I spoke to told me it'd been common knowledge for years that he was coming on to his students, but he'd always tell everyone that it was the kid coming on to him. He'd be believed, she'd be punished, and it was usually enough to stop others from saying anything. This last time he didn't allow for modern technology. A friend of the pupil was crouched outside filming the whole thing on their phone. No wriggle room there."

Ethan tried to hide his interest, this account seemed to gel with Carrie's second telling of the incident. Again, it felt as though her lies were woven around the truth.

Cal continued, "I can't find the brother anywhere, and so far I haven't picked up any trace of Mum either. I also tried to speak with Dad but he wasn't having a bar of it. Told me to go copulate in no uncertain terms."

He gave a self-deprecating grin, "I should be hurt at how many people hate us journalists."

Ethan chuckled, "Hmm, maybe because most of you are muckraking arseholes?"

Cal raised his pint as though saluting him, "Hey, I resemble that remark."

Ethan returned to the subject, "So, anything else interesting crop up about our Carrie?"

The journalist gave a sniff, "We're still driving down that one-way street then? Actually, I'm on the lookout for the mother, Mandy. She might have a tale to tell if we can find her. Local rumours suggest she went into rehab but that doesn't seem to explain why she's not shown up again in the last fifteen years. I'll keep digging for her though, I'm not one to quit at the first hurdle!"

That gave Ethan a cold shiver, it did seem odd that a mother would never come back and try and reconnect with her children. Hopefully, Cal wouldn't end up digging her up literally. How was this whole family so damaged? Mum an alcoholic who'd run off when her kids were small, the son in a secure hospital, and their daughter in prison for murder. The only one that seemed settled was Stan, or was he? Was there something dark under the surface that Ethan had missed when he first spoke to him?

'Who else are you planning to speak to?"

Cal sighed, "I'm running out of interesting options, it's as though the whole town has closed down around what happened. There's the usual attention-seeking suspects who can't wait to talk about Carrie whilst claiming to have known her well. Most of them are just ex-pupils from the same schools and I doubt they said more than good morning to her for the whole time they "knew" her."

"Worth a try though, you never know, we might end up with at least one useful bit of information out of it."

'The journalist narrowed his eyes, "Why can't I help but think you've got your own agenda already set up, and that you've got no intention of sharing it with me?"

Ethan shrugged, "That'll be your suspicious mind telling you porkies. If I didn't know better I might even call you paranoid..."

Cal shook his head and chuckled, "Never bother trying to argue with a psychiatrist!"

Smiling at Cal he felt a little guilty. He *was* holding back and he did have his own agenda. He wanted to hear what the other kids who'd known her at school had to say. Was Carrie the shy bookish child who rebelled as a teenager as she'd told him? What about the hints from her primary school teacher that she'd been unpopular and "sly." Maybe the truth lay somewhere in between. The deeper he went the more convinced he was becoming that there was something hidden, something dark.

Cal swirled the amber liquid around his glass thoughtfully.

"Something about this feels strange. Obviously, I don't know as much as you do, but just from the look on your face I'm getting the idea that this isn't as simple as I thought when I took the story on."

He started to look excited as it sank in.

"This could be huge, one of those big stories that make my career."

Ethan threw him a dirty look, "Remember that's my patient you're talking about. She's not just a story Cal. I need to get to the bottom of it before I write a report that could effectively either keep her in prison or release her into the community. If I get this wrong it's serious."

The journalist nodded, "Sorry, you're right, I do have a tendency to get carried away. I know there's a real-life behind every story, and I do appreciate your help with this."

Ethan smiled to let him know his apology was accepted, but it had made him think. Was he taking too much of a risk working with Cal? This job was important to him and he was currently doing things that could mean instant dismissal. The problem was, he couldn't shake the urge to dig into the system again to look for Carrie's mum.

She must be out there somewhere, and maybe she held the key to all of this.

Chapter Fifteen

Carrie looked pale, her eyes wide as she fidgeted with the hems of her sleeves. She sat down awkwardly as though it pained her to do so, in fact, she even winced slightly. Cocking her head to one side as though waiting for him to ask, Ethan wondered if it was worth ignoring her obvious bid for attention. Curiosity got the better of him, plus the good manners that his parents had drummed into him.

"Is everything okay Carrie?"

The woman shook her head and dipped her eyes to the table as though afraid to look at him directly.

"It doesn't matter Dr Quinn. I'll be fine in a day or so."

There was clearly a story behind her physical appearance, and now she'd tantalised him with it he found himself needing to hear the whole thing.

"Of course, it matters Carrie, you look as though you're in pain. What happened?"

More tugging on the threads of her already ragged cardigan. He'd noticed that Carrie dressed for the mood she presented him with. Shabby clothes that had seen better days for the anxious Carrie, and smarter, slightly sexy attire when she was bursting with confidence. He was starting to see a pattern and a routine to her behaviour and presentation. She almost donned the clothes, and expression, and exhibited the body language to fit her narrative.

"Some of the other prisoners have taken exception to the idea that I was involved in what Olive did to herself. I don't like to make accusations but with the way the staff talk about me it was only a matter of time before it became common knowledge on the wing."

Ethan waited to see if she added anything, but when she resumed staring at the table top he gently prompted her without feeding into the accusation she'd made about the staff.

"Did someone hurt you, Carrie? All assaults should be reported to one of the officers on your wing, would you like me to tell them what happened?"

Carrie gave a small nod and replied in a small, frightened voice.

"I didn't see who did it, they crept up on me on the way to the showers and hit me in the back with someone hard. It's usually a stolen snooker ball in a sock. I can't see but I think I'm badly bruised."

Clever, thought Ethan cynically, not being able to name anyone means she isn't grassing, and can't be found out if it isn't true. It also gives her an opening to accuse the staff of being responsible.

"I'll be passing this on to the staff and asking them to keep a closer eye on you in the communal areas."

Carrie thanked him in a voice tinged with relief, then she scrunched up her brow as though worried again.

"And what about the way they talk about me? It wouldn't be so bad but they don't keep it in the office. The whole wing knows that they think I caused Olive to hurt herself. I didn't you know."

Ethan was pretty sure this had been her main objective. Paying back the staff for their suspicions and dislike of her, and he was the tool she intended to use.

"I'll try and raise that sensitively. We wouldn't want to make things worse so it'll need to be handled carefully."

He wasn't sure, but he thought he saw the smallest smirk pass over her lips before she resumed the anxious face. Just to ensure he realised how bad it was she wriggled on the chair and gave a sharp intake of breath at the pain the movement caused her.

Deciding that a change of topic was in order, Ethan moved along to encouraging her to share some more of her history with him.

"Tell me more about your job at the library. Did you enjoy working there and how did that lead you to the role as a teaching assistant?"

Carrie looked taken aback at the subject change. Perhaps she'd been hoping not to have to face any more questions about her past by gaining his sympathy.

"I enjoyed it. I've always loved books and reading so it was a dream come true to be in a workplace surrounded by them. It was just me and the head librarian most days, although we did have a few volunteers who came in to help organise the books. When I told Mrs Mayhew the head librarian about how I'd always wanted to teach she put me in charge of reading to the children when they came in."

Carrie looked far away as though reliving the whole thing in her head. There was a small smile playing on her lips and Ethan thought it was the happiest he'd seen her so far. Maybe this had been a good time in her life, and if so it was more likely that she'd tell him the truth about it.

"I loved holding the reading groups, and the little ones were so enthusiastic to learn it was a pleasure to help them. That was how I came to hear about the teaching assistant role. The teacher who bought them over each week told me and encouraged me to apply. She said I was just what they were looking for. Mrs. Mayhew could see I wasn't sure and she reminded me that it was a step closer to my goal of being a teacher. I applied and was lucky enough to get the job."

Carrie sat up straighter, and although this made her wince again she seemed more comfortable than earlier.

"I was so lucky to have so many supportive people around me to make up for my father's lack of interest."

Ethan nodded while thinking about how she'd slipped that in as though validating her own claims. Carrie sighed deeply and gave a small sniff as though holding back tears.

"I wish I'd had a chance to thank them, but I doubt I ever will now."

The questioning look she gave him suggested she was digging for a clue on what his report would suggest so Ethan ignored it. He noticed her eyes narrow in annoyance before she replaced her mask of innocence.

Ethan kept the conversation to less controversial topics for the remainder of their session. Carrie's responses were perfunctory and she seemed very distracted. He wondered what it was that was playing on her mind. Was she worried about how close they were getting to addressing her actual offence, or was it more that she didn't like moving away from topics she had control of?

On the wing the officers were having handover so Ethan waited outside the office until they'd done. He noticed a few of the inmates were eying him with interest as they walked by. Most of them were on his caseload, and he had a basic idea of their risk levels. There was the small woman with the angelic face who'd stabbed her boyfriend over a hundred times for cheating on her. Lisa shot him a wide smile that made her childlike face light up – if you didn't know better you'd think she was sweet and innocent – but Ethan knew better. Lisa had a temper and was prone to outbursts of violence, her strength belied her small stature and she won most of the fights she took on.

Interestingly he noticed Carrie approach Lisa and put an affectionate arm around her shoulder. Lisa flinched slightly but when Carrie whispered in her ear she relaxed, and even laughed quietly. At that point, Carrie looked up and caught him watching. Her irritation was quickly hidden but Ethan saw it before she hid it.

"What can we do for you, Dr Quinn?"

Rachel was leaning around the office door and Ethan moved closer so he could keep the conversation between them.

"I need a quick chat about Carrie. Some information she passed on that I feel needs to be shared with you."

Rachel rolled her eyes but invited him into the office and closed the door behind him. Leaning against the counter she waited for him to start.

"Carrie has disclosed that she was physically assaulted on the way to the showers. She's saying she didn't see who it was but thinks they hit her in the small of her back with a snooker ball in a sock."

Rachel smirked, "That old wive's tale. We count all the balls and there's no chance anyone could sneak one out and use it. So, why does she think she was a victim of this sudden attack on her person?"

Ethan paused, he wasn't entirely comfortable sharing Carrie's accusation that the staff had caused it by talking about her.

"She thinks the other prisoners blame her for what Olive did to herself."

That made a few of the officers snort and chuckle to themselves, but it was Rachel who answered.

"Why does she think that? We've not heard any whispers and usually we would. It's just Carrie attention seeking, she wants you to feel sorry for her and by the looks of it she's hit just the right note too."

Ethan frowned, he could understand that the staff weren't keen to think an assault had happened under their noses, but there was no need to speak to him like he was a gullible idiot.

"I think I'd know if I was being played for a fool Rachel. I'm well aware that as a team you aren't keen on Carrie, I'm also aware that she has a history of not telling the truth. I'm not telling you this is a fact, I'm simply passing it on so you're aware."

Rachel, clearly realising she'd pushed her luck with Ethan, gave him an apologetic smile.

"Sorry Dr Quinn, that didn't come out as I'd intended. As you say Carrie is often economical with the truth so it makes it difficult for us to know when to believe her or not. You can rest assured that we'll look into this assault and keep a closer eye on Carrie to make sure nothing else happens to her."

Ethan felt he had to be satisfied with that, it was probably the best he was going to get from the team. Nodding and thanking them he hurried back to his office.

Chapter Sixteen

Cal had come up trumps with finding Mrs Donna Mayhew, the retired librarian. She'd agreed to meet with them, and in person, Ethan had found she looked exactly how he imagined she would. Despite being in her eighties she was sprightly, bright-eyed, and held her back ramrod straight. She hadn't been keen to speak to a journalist, but once Cal promised not to use anything she said without her written permission she'd seemed more comfortable.

"Carrie hadn't long left school when she came to work at the library. To be honest I was surprised to get her application. She wasn't one of our bookworms and they're usually the type to apply for any jobs that come up. We didn't have many applicants and Carrie was well-spoken, articulate, and interested so I offered her the job. At first, she was everything she'd promised to be, presentable, polite, and on time. Once she had her feet under the table it was as though she'd had a personality transplant. Suddenly she was surly, unhelpful, and always late arriving for work. An example would be when I explained that it was part of her role to do the reading with the school group each week. You've never seen someone make such a sour face. Stropping and complaining that she didn't like small children. No one was as shocked as me when she left us to take up a post as a teaching assistant."

Another twist to Carrie's version of events, Ethan thought. What was the reason behind this lie though? Did she think it painted her in a better light?

"Was there anything else that you remember that might help me understand her a bit better?"

The retired teacher looked as though she was weighing up if she should continue before answering.

"This isn't anything I could ever prove, but I believed that Carrie was behind some cruel pranks. If I spoke to her sharply about lateness or her lack of a work ethic something strange would always happen not long after. Someone would key my car, my favourite plant in the garden would die, or things would be moved at work so I had to spend ages looking for them."

Ethan frowned, this sounded similar to the description from her teacher, but he also had to consider that anything he heard now was through the lens of hindsight. People often used what they knew now to change how they viewed what happened in the past.

"Did you know Carrie's younger brother?"

Mrs Mayhew smiled at what appeared to be a pleasant memory.

"Dan was always in the library, he loved books and spent hours poking through the shelves looking for something new to read. I haven't seen him for a long time though, I think he might have moved away after..well, after what happened with his sister."

Mrs. Mayhew seemed reluctant to say the word murder, Ethan was also interested that she seemed to think Dan had moved away. Had his slide into schizophrenia been so sudden that no one had noticed? It wasn't as though he could bring it up without breaching Dan's right to privacy but it was something else to file away in the box of things he needed to look into.

Ethan tried to concentrate on the film he'd put on the tele but realized that he'd been so lost in thought he hadn't taken in hardly any of it so far. All he could think about was Carrie. The more he got to know about her past the stranger it all seemed. A small, but persistent, voice in the back of his head kept reminding him of all the inconsistencies with her story. He'd just given up on trying to ignore his thoughts when his phone rang and dragged him back to reality. It was the prison, Rachel sounded shaken as she explained they'd had another serious incident and he was needed on the wing. She rang off without sharing the details, and Ethan tried to imagine what'd happened as he snatched up his keys and pulled on his shoes.

At the prison, he was hurried through security by a more sour than ever Croft, who barely looked at him let alone spoke. He tried a few times to get her to fill him in on what he was walking into but her refusal to engage was absolute.

"I'll let the staff on the wing fill you in doctor, it ain't my place to."

That was clearly all he was going to get out of her, and since he was only a few steps away from Robin wing he might as well wait until he spoke to Rachel in person. On the wing the noise was overwhelming.

Following the protocol everyone had been locked up to keep them away from the incident while the officers tried to deal with it. Blood spattered the walls and floors and a chunky chair leg smeared red lay in the middle of the corridor. Three of the staff were trying to restrain someone, and another two were crouched over a large still figure crumpled in the middle of the worst of the blood.

"Get your fucking hands off me!"

The squeaky, childlike voice was distinctive enough that Ethan immediately recognised that it belonged to Lisa Caldwell. Rachel tugged him into the office where they watched the incident continue to unfold from behind the safety of the plexiglass. Rachel filled him in while her fingers drummed impatiently on the office desk.

"We think it was premeditated but we have no idea why. Lisa broke a leg off one of the chairs and then crouched behind a door until Pepper Andrews went by. She jumped her, smashing at her with the chair leg. She's so small she had to jump up to get to her face, we've never seen anything like it. She'd done a lot of damage by the time we managed to restrain her. Pepper's in a really bad way, an ambulance has just arrived but her face is a mess."

Rachel shuddered, and Ethan thought how bad it must've been to unnerve a guard who'd seen it all before. The paramedics came at a run, but slowed right down when they saw the state of the woman lying in a pool of congealing blood. One of them bent over her before looking at his colleague and shaking his head. Ethan glanced around the wing, the other officers had all stopped still and were looking at the still figure on the floor. Even Lisa had stopped wriggling and fighting, her legs gave way, and she would've crumpled to the floor if the guards hadn't been holding her up.

Looking at her pale face Ethan couldn't help but think about how he'd seen Carrie whispering in her ear earlier. Had she somehow goaded Lisa into attacking a fellow inmate, and if so, why?

The area was a crime scene so Pepper had to be left where she was. That meant the prisoners were going to be confined to their rooms until the communal area had been processed and cleaned. Usually, this would've created chaos, prisoners banging and shouting and demanding to be let out. Instead, there was an eerie quiet broken only by the sound of the paramedics moving around as they waited for the police to arrive. Since Lisa was already in custody she'd be contained in a single segregation cell elsewhere in the prison.

Rachel, who was still pale and shaken, explained the protocol to Ethan in the office.

"All unexpected deaths in custody are referred to the coroner and investigated by the police so this one is definitely going that route. Lisa will stay in seg and the police will interview her here at the prison and then she'll face the appropriate charges. As you know, Lisa has a diagnosis of borderline personality disorder so you or Dr Edwards will need to assess if she's fit for interview."

Ethan thought of the sessions he'd previously had with Lisa. As he hadn't been in post long, and had been tied up with Carrie's report, their appointments had been less frequent than he'd usually have them with a new patient. He'd found her to be disarmingly blunt and honest. They'd only scratched the surface of her background, but even the little he knew suggested some intense childhood traumas. He'd felt that with Lisa being so open, and that she was finally saying she wanted to get herself straight on the outside, she stood a good chance of a positive outcome. Now it was likely that she'd never see the outside again.

"I'll speak to her. I'm here anyway so I may as well be the one to assess her."

Rachel nodded, "I was hoping you'd volunteer. Dr Edwards is a great doctor, but Lisa didn't really hit it off with him."

Ethan managed a smile despite the seriousness of the situation as he remembered the notes he'd read in Lisa's file.

"I read the reports, apparently she took great pleasure in mocking his baldness and calling him "the little bald man."

Rachel gave a chuckle, "He wasn't exactly her biggest fan after that."

Picking up her keys she jerked her head towards the office door, "No time like the present. At least when the police arrive we'll already have an idea of if she's fit for them to question."

Ethan followed her out of the wing. They were heading into the main prison, and since he'd not been there before he was struck by how different it was to Robin Wing. It was the noise that hit him first. Shouting, singing, crying, and repeated banging sounds. The crashing and clattering of various gates being opened and closed was the background theme tune to the rest of the sounds. There was also the smells. The heavy smell of cannabis and an underlying sickly sweetness suggested some prisoners were using crack. Overlying this was the stench of boiled food, unwashed bodies, and cleaning fluids. It was overwhelming, and made Ethan realise how fortunate he was that he was allocated to Robin Wing.

Seg was located downstairs away from the wings which meant it was quieter down there. Lisa had calmed down by now. The guards had stripped her and replaced her blood-soaked clothes with a prison-issue tracksuit that was two sizes too big for her small frame. She hadn't been allowed to clean herself as the police would want to document the blood splatter that was the only colour on her otherwise pasty face.

Lisa was hunched on the bare bedframe, her back against the wall and her knees drawn up to her chest. She looked like a small child who'd been sent to their room after being naughty, and Ethan felt a wave of sadness at what lay ahead for this damaged, vulnerable woman. Rachel had explained it was unlikely she'd be allowed back to Robin Wing so she'd be in general population. That meant limited access to mental health support, and the high possibility that other prisoners would exploit her. She'd get worse as time went on, and eventually, she'd be unrecognisable as the woman he'd first assessed only a couple of weeks ago.

Rachel was reluctant to leave him alone with her, "She's only just caved in someone's face with a chair leg Doc."

Ethan had waved off her concerns, "And look at her now, does she appear hostile and violent? She'll be exhausted, emotionally and physically, but if for any reason she does kick off, I'll use the buzzer."

Shrugging, Rachel left them alone, and with one final look through the peep hatch, he'd heard her footsteps as she walked further up the corridor to wait for him. Ethan couldn't see a place to sit until Lisa was considered lower risk she wasn't even allowed a chair in the room. Not wanting to stand over her he sat on the floor halfway between the bed and the exit.

"What happened Lisa?"

She turned slowly toward his voice, her eyes red and puffy from crying as she sniffed and wiped her sleeve across her face.

"Dunno Doc. I just got it in my head that Pepper was after me, and before long all I could think was "kill or be killed." As soon as I saw what I'd done I went into shock."

"Where did you get the idea that she was after you from?"

If Ethan was hoping Lisa would link Carrie to anything he was going to be disappointed as she shrugged in reply. He caught a flash of fear before she ducked her head so he couldn't see her face.

"Maybe I've started hearing voices Doc, because I'm sure it was a voice that told me to hurt Pepper."

Lisa was aware of how things worked. She'd been inside more often than she'd been out, and before that, she'd grown up in the care system. If she could get it logged that she was psychotic at the time she'd be hoping for a bed in hospital rather than a cell in the prison. They talked for a bit longer as Ethan tested her awareness of time, place, and person. She showed no signs of being floridly unwell, and she didn't express any delusional ideation. Much as it pained him to give her the all-clear he had no reason to block a police interview. In an ideal world, Ethan would've recommended Lisa was transferred to a secure unit, but with beds few and far between there wouldn't be one for someone who wasn't actively psychotic.

Lisa was going to be lost in the system, and Ethan couldn't help feeling a dragging sense of loss at the thought of it. There was also a spark of anger, if she had been prompted by Carrie then the woman had a lot to answer for. He'd just got up to press the call bell for Rachel when he heard a key turning in the lock. It was Rachel, but she wasn't alone, a large man with a stony face was standing just behind her. Ethan noticed the way his eyes wandered and took everything in. Police, he realised, just as Rachel introduced him.

"DCI Greggs has just arrived, and wants to know if the prisoner is fit for interview."

Ethan glanced sadly at Lisa before nodding his head, "Yes detective, she's fit to be interviewed, but please take her mental health into account. Lisa can be very fragile underneath what you see on the surface."

DCI Greggs made a face that suggested he couldn't care a less about Lisa's fragility but nodded back as though agreeing. Ethan could see Rachel was waiting for him, and with one final look at Lisa, he followed her out.

Chapter Seventeen

C arrie had on her childlike persona today. Her clothes were baggy and comfortable, and she swung her legs back and forth while she sat on the chair like a small girl trying to get a swing to work. Occasionally she glanced at the blinking camera in the corner of the room as though checking it was on and recording her.

Ethan decided to go straight in with the incident and try and gauge an unplanned reaction from her.

"I'm sure you've heard about the incident between Lisa and Pepper earlier."

Carrie's face drooped into an expression of sadness and she wiped her finger under her dry eye as though catching an imaginary tear.

"Yes doctor, it was terrible. Poor Pepper."

Insincerity shone from every pore and Ethan decided to see how she reacted to the additional information the staff had come across.

"The officers have spoken to everyone on the wing and it would appear that Pepper was the prisoner responsible for attacking you."

Carrie's mouth formed a perfect O shape of surprise, and Ethan remembered how the staff had put it when they'd updated him.

"Apparently it was common knowledge that Pepper had it in for Carrie. Her own kids were taken into care when she was given a custodial and she notoriously hates any prisoner who's in here for harming kids. She bided her time, and eventually, when she had the chance to go for Carrie she took it. We suspect Carrie knows exactly who it was. We can't prove it, but it'd be just like her to get someone else to do her dirty work for her."

The Carrie he was faced with looked as though butter wouldn't melt in her mouth, but he'd seen her whispering in Lisa's ear himself. The problem was if he took that to the staff they'd be quick to jump on Carrie having done something. He knew they already disliked her and it wouldn't take much to cause that to escalate even more. He had no evidence it wasn't just the casual conversation that Carrie had insisted it'd been.

"Did you know Lisa very well?"

Carrie gave a half smile at the change of direction, "Are you asking because you think I had something to do with the way she kicked off? I saw how you looked at me when I was speaking to her the other day."

Ethan smiled back, "Just a simple question so I know how much support you might need. If she's a good friend of yours it'll have been more impactful than if the two of you weren't close."

Carrie narrowed her eyes as though still suspicious of his motives, but she answered with a careless shrug.

"Not especially well. I tend to try and not mix with the other inmates, but she was less hostile than the others in my experience."

Considering Lisa had a reputation for being aggressive and lashing out that wasn't a description he'd expected. Deciding not to challenge her on it he moved back to her past.

"Let's leave that incident and go back to our usual sessions. Can you tell me a bit more about your relationship with your brother and what you remember of your mother?"

She paused and closed her eyes as though trying to remember back through the mists of time.

Carrie

I'm guessing that you want honesty from me and I'm going to try my best. Growing up, secrets were the currency of the realm in my family. We weren't allowed to share the details of our lives so we created new stories that eventually got repeated so often it was hard to remember what was and wasn't real.

My father is a man who likes his family to present to the world as perfect so he can hide behind the fantasy. My mother drank, and I imagine that was her hiding place from the reality of living with Stan. He dominated and controlled our lives, from what we wore to what food was put on the table. We all had our positions in his world and I was fortunate enough to be considered the "favourite." Dan on the other hand was at the bottom of the pile. Quiet and constantly terrified of his own shadow, my father despised his weakness while he encouraged me to be bold, and as devious as I needed to be to get my own way. I was taught to treat my mother and brother with the same contempt and disregard that he did. It was easy to fall into our roles, my mother cowed and drunk, and my brother, who disappeared into himself until there was nothing but a shadow of the boy he once was. My father liked it that way, he knew where he stood with us all and his kingdom was exactly as he wanted it to be.

My untruth to you about my mother wasn't born of my need to lie in our sessions, it was simply the version we'd been told to use when asked about her. Mandy Martins walked out on us without so much as a backward glance. The first we knew of her leaving was when no one arrived to collect us from school. I stood with Dan in the cold. Autumn leaves swirled around our ankles as we strained to see far enough up the street to catch a glimpse of her. Mum was regularly late for pick-up. By the time we finished school in the afternoon, she'd put in a hard day's drinking and often lost track of time. Our teacher didn't seem concerned at first, but eventually, we were herded back into the warmth of the school while they called our father to collect us.

He was livid, as angry as I'd ever seen him and I remember feeling a little afraid of what would happen when we got home and he found her passed out on the sofa. Last time he'd locked her in the house for a week and made her give up drinking cold turkey. I thought she was going to die, and despite my attitude towards her she was still my mother and I didn't want to lose her forever like that.

Our house was dark and cold. No one had put the heating or the lights on, and there was no smell of food coming from the kitchen to suggest that Mum had started our tea. My dad went from room to room, flinging open doors and yelling her name. It wasn't until he tried their room that he found enough of her clothes missing to realise that she'd gone.

He cooked our tea and we ate in silence as it sank in that she probably wasn't coming back. It was when we'd finished eating that

Dad announced that we were to tell anyone who asked that she was dead.

"Say it enough times kids and it'll feel like the truth. Besides, she may as well be for all the use she is to us."

I'll never forget his words because they struck me as summing up the situation perfectly and from that day onwards she was dead. Dan took it the hardest. He was the one she doted on and fussed over and with her gone, he had no one. It was me and my dad with Dan nothing more than a silent ghost that we had to feed and clean up after.

For me, he stopped existing many years before he really did. I have no idea where he is now, he was just a teenager the last time I saw him. I can't imagine he made much of himself as an adult though.

My father ruled the roost and we all did as we were told without question. So long as we played our roles he was content, and when he was content we didn't have to face his wrath. It was the same with how he wanted us viewed from the outside. We were supposed to be perfect examples of what a wonderful single father he was. Anything, or any-one, that threatened that image needed dealing with. Children who bullied or mocked me at school, teachers who picked on me, or anyone who criticised me were seen as a reflection on him. He encouraged me to pay them back and show them that I wasn't someone to be messed with, and when I couldn't he'd do it. Nasty tricks like pushing poo through someone's letterbox, keying a car, or setting them up were the usual methods. I became quite good at it and very rarely got caught out.

It wasn't healthy, but it was our form of normal and I didn't know any different until I ended up here. Surrounded by other inmates from dysfunctional families I can see how our pasts influence who we become.

• • • ● ● • ● ● • • •

When she'd done Carrie leaned back in the chair as though waiting for his approval. He noticed that she'd used a lot of terms that would ring true for him. Ethan ran the story through his head, it appeared on the surface that she was finally telling him the truth, but something still didn't ring true about it. Was Stan so clever that he could fool Ethan into not recognising him as the psychopath that Carrie described?

She was clearly suggesting that her relationship with lying was taught at her father's knee, but was it yet another of Carrie's masks to hide from the reality of what she'd done? She had the details text book perfect. That was exactly how a psychopath would behave. Seeing his children as extensions of himself, and playing favourites to split the family so he was always in control, those were commonly seen behaviours. Ethan was almost grateful when the guards arrived to take Carrie back to the wing. He wasn't sure he could've continued to talk to her as usual with all the questions he had flying around in his head.

With this new information he knew he had to speak to Carrie's mother, and there was only one way to find Mandy Martins, another unofficial look through the system.

It didn't take long to get a hit.

Mandy had been checked into a rehab placement around the time she left her family. There was nothing on the system to show where she'd been since, but most interesting was the note of who signed her into the unit all those years ago. Stan Martin. The man who'd then left his children standing outside school waiting for a mother he knew wouldn't be showing up. Unbelievably he'd then put on a show of searching the house for her before announcing to the children that she'd left them and "may as well be dead."

If all of this was true the man was a monster. An unfeeling psychopath who'd dumped his wife in rehab, and then tormented his own children with her loss.

Chapter Eighteen

Ethan had considered messaging Cal but then decided he'd rather go alone. There was more chance of getting what he needed without a journalist with him. He made the two-hour drive straight after work to Carrie's maternal nan because he was pretty sure she'd know where Mandy was.

Iris Lewis's bungalow was situated in the middle of a housing estate surrounded by blocks of flats. As Ethan got out of his car a young man in his twenties approached as if he'd been hovering around nearby just waiting for someone to arrive. He bounced on the balls of his feet as he walked giving him a strange, rocking gait, and when he smiled he gave Ethan a view of his rotted teeth. Twitching and fidgeting as he looked everywhere but at Ethan directly he'd started to hold out his hand when a voice yelled from the direction of the bungalow.

"Oi, Pothole. Leave the man alone."

The young man with the strange name jumped as though the words had physically hit him, before wordlessly spinning on his heel and bouncing back to wherever he'd been lurking when Ethan had arrived.

The woman who'd shouted was small and neatly turned out, she eyed Ethan suspiciously as he approached.

"Mrs Lewis? I'm Dr Ethan Quinn and I was hoping you could spare me a few minutes of your time."

The woman nodded briskly, acknowledging that she was Mrs Lewis, but the suspicious look remained.

"What do you want Dr Quinn?"

Ethan felt, rather than saw, that he'd become the focus of everyone's attention around the estate. He couldn't see anyone watching, but eyes bore into him from behind the net curtains up and down the street.

"Can we talk inside please?"

Mrs Lewis gave him an up-and-down look before narrowing her eyes and stepping back to give him access.

"I'm tougher than I look so no funny business young man."

Ethan hid a grin as he agreed to behave himself. The house was as neat as the woman herself. Not a speck of dust dared to linger on the surfaces, and the carpet was lined with fresh vacuum tracks. Ethan accepted the offer of tea and waited patiently until Mrs Lewis returned with a tray of tea things. Setting it down on the table she took her time pouring out the drinks.

"Thank you for intervening with young Pothole earlier, strange name."

Ethan tried for an icebreaker and was rewarded with a smile, "We call him Pothole because everyone tries their best to avoid him. He's always on the scrounge, and I was pretty sure he was about to try his luck with you."

Sitting in an armchair opposite him she sipped her tea and gave a sigh of enjoyment.

"So, what's this about, as if I couldn't guess?"

"I'm the doctor tasked with writing a report to decide if your granddaughter, Carrie, should be considered for parole. I'm trying to speak to her family to get some background so I'm looking for her mother, Mandy."

Mrs Lewis looked away as she considered what he'd just said.

"Call me Iris. I had a feeling it was about Carrie, she's been banged up for more than fifteen years hasn't she?"

Ethan nodded and waited for her to continue.

"I'm not keen on the idea doctor. Mandy was badly damaged by the years she spent married to that prick Stan, and it took me a long time to get her settled. She goes by her maiden name now, she's left all of that behind and if we're going to rake it up I need a damn good reason why."

Iris's face was set with a stubborn expression that suggested it would take a hell of a lot of explaining to get around her. Ethan could tell he wasn't likely to make a good enough case to excuse the potential damage he could do by opening old wounds. What was he doing anyway? How would it help his report to swing a wrecking ball through Mandy Martin's life like this?

"I'll speak to him, mum."

A thin, delicate-looking woman had appeared in the room and was addressing Iris. Ethan could see Carrie in her features and in her mannerisms. Iris sighed and shook her head.

"You don't have to Mandy. Dr Quinn can easily write up his report without you ripping yourself open for him. You haven't seen the girl in decades so I can't see how you've got much to add to it."

Ethan blushed, that basically summed up what he'd just been thinking himself. He shifted uncomfortably on the chair and considered the most dignified way to make his exit.

"I'm fine mum, none of this can hurt me now and I think the doctor should have a better idea of what Carrie was like as a child. If she's as good at lying now as she was then, I can't see him having much in the way of real information to go on. It's not as though Stan would tell him anything helpful either."

Iris looked away for a moment as though composing herself before getting to her feet.

"I've got things to be getting on with so I'll leave you to it."

She swept out of the room aiming a look at Ethan as she went that passed on the unspoken message that he wasn't to push her daughter too hard. Mandy took her mother's seat and poured the last of the pot into her mug. She took her time adding sugar and milk, and Ethan noticed a slight tremor in her hand. She smiled weakly at him and gave a sad sigh.

"I'm nervous doctor, I'm always nervous. My mother would tell you I live on my nerves. I've not been the same since I met Stan, he ruined me and I'll never trust another man again."

Wincing slightly as she adjusted her slight figure in the chair she sipped from her cup and began her story.

I was only 17 when I met Stan. Along with my group of friends, we'd sneak into a local club where he was the doorman. If we gave him a flash of our legs he'd let us in, so we took to wearing short skirts and piling on the make-up. He took a special shine to me, and being young and stupid I enjoyed the attention. He'd buy me drinks and invite me out back for a smoke with him. Stan was clever, he was never creepy or touchy-feely. He just chatted with me about stuff and made me feel as though he was interested in everything I had to say. Eventually, we started going out, and when Stan got me in the family way he seemed really pleased. I'd fretted for days about how to tell him, I thought he'd go mad and dump me and I'd be one of those single mothers. Looking back I wish he had, I can't see I'd have messed it up as much on my own.

It felt as though I had no control over anything from that day on. The wedding was planned and agreed on and Stan told me I should give up working to concentrate on making a home for our child. He put down the deposit on a nice little house and we moved straight in after the wedding. I thought it would look ungrateful to complain, so I just went along with everything. Stan choose the decor, the furniture, and even the baby's name, I had no say in anything.

Carrie was a difficult baby, she didn't go through the night until after she started school, and I was exhausted. Night after relentless night I paced the floors with her in my arms, willing her to go to sleep. It was almost as though she was intentionally torturing me. I was like a zombie most of the time, and it wasn't long before Stan started complaining. I smelled like baby vomit, I hadn't lost the pregnancy weight, and there was nothing decent made for his supper. It never occurred to him to actually help me. Bringing up the kids was woman's work and in his view, I was failing in my only job.

I didn't have the energy to argue with him, I could barely manage to brush my teeth every day let alone put together an argument. Stan thrived while I was like that. He took pleasure in humiliating me in front of people by pointing out my faults, and he'd make me feel like a shitty mother. If Carrie was crying he'd pluck her out of my arms, and she'd stop the minute he held her. It was as though she'd already joined forces with him from the day she arrived in the world.

That's when the drinking started. At first, it was just a couple of glasses of wine to relax me in the evening, then I'd have one at lunchtime just to get through the afternoon. Soon, I was splashing vodka in my OJ in the mornings, and drinking the whole day. Carrie had already started school when I fell pregnant with Dan. Stan might have thought I was a dirty, fat mess, but that didn't stop him from taking what he felt was his right in the marital bed. This time it was different. Despite the drinking, I felt more able to manage, and Dan was such an easy baby. He rarely cried, and he went through the night after only a few weeks.

I think Stan had hoped I'd fall apart more when I had the two of them, and he despised Dan for being so close to me. It was the other way around this time, when he held Dan he'd scream, and reach out for me, and Stan hated it. By now Carrie was his little shadow, following him around the house and treating me with the same disgust as her father.

She'd always told lies, but I'd convinced myself it was the usual get yourself out of trouble ones that most children tell. She'd look at me with those big blue eyes of hers and announce "I didn't do it." Even if you caught her red-handed, she'd never own up. Then she started telling stories at school, making out like I was a bad mother to her. I know I drank, I'm not saying I didn't, but her dad would tell me he was going to collect her and then not show up. Course, the school would call me and it would look as though I hadn't turned up. Carrie would play along with her big sad eyes and insist that mummy was coming for her.

It wasn't just the lies either. She was sly. If anyone upset her she'd spend weeks planning how to get her own back, I'd never known a child be as fixated on revenge as her. Carrie was smart with it too, she rarely got caught out, but I'd know, I'd always know. I was her mother, and I could see underneath the lies. She was her father's daughter alright.

When Stan put me in rehab he said it was to fix me up so I could come home and be a better mum to the kids. Turns out that was my marching orders. As soon as we'd signed the papers he dumped all my stuff round my mum's and told her to tell me not to come back. I tried once, I was desperate to see Dan and I hung around the school waiting to see him on his first day. Stan caught sight of me, and once Dan had gone in, came over. He made out he wanted to talk and we went for a drive. He parked up near the cliffs and then dragged me to the edge. He said if I showed my face again he'd drop me over the side.

"The kids already think you're dead so it won't matter if you really are."

He left me there to walk home. It was miles and then it started raining. By the time I got back, I was soaked through and barely had the energy to get through the front door. By the time my mum had come home, I'd drank my way through everything she had in the house. Even the sherry from Christmas. Mum pulled me back together, and she supported me to get dry again, and eventually, I became what you see before you. A ghost. A half-woman who lost her children and was too much of a coward to fight for them.

• • • ● ● • ● • • •

Mandy looked wiped by the time she'd finished, and Ethan felt a twang of guilt at putting her through it. She looked as fragile as a china doll and just as pale. Ethan had noted that she described Carrie as a difficult baby whilst her father had said she was easy – who was right or were they both right based on their personal experiences with her?

"I know where Carrie is and what she did, but what about my Dan? Do you know where he is?"

Ethan sighed, this wasn't going to be easy, "I'm so sorry Mandy, he's in a psychiatric hospital and has been for some time now."

He avoided adding that Dan had gone in there not long after his sister was convicted of the murder of three children. Mandy worked it out for herself though.

"I expect all that business with his sister ruined him. He was always the sensitive one and it must've broken him to know his sister was capable of that. She'll have got it from her dad, children are like a blank sheet of paper until someone writes on it, and it was her dad who wrote her story for her."

Ethan liked the picture that created, but he was in two minds as to whether he agreed or not. It came down to the age-old question of nurture or nature, and Ethan had seen evidence of both over the years. While many offenders were created by their environments, backgrounds, and past trauma, many others appeared to have no reason for what they did. Seemingly ordinary families could suddenly discover a psychopath in their midst. He'd seen the confusion and watched as they asked themselves what they'd done wrong.

The answer was – nothing.

Every now and again, nature threw a spanner in the works in the form of a child who grew up to commit the most horrific crimes despite, rather than because, of their upbringing. Was that the case with Carrie, or had her environment shaped her from an early age? Her mother was quick to point the finger at Carrie's father, but then other people around at the time believed he'd done the best he could as a single parent. Much as he sensed no deception from Mandy, she was still an ex-addict and maybe she was seeing the past through the lens of her addiction. Despite his failings as a husband, he had no evidence that Stan hadn't been the best father he could be. Everyone he'd spoken to had their own agenda or reasons to blame each other, and it was hard for Ethan to see which one was telling the truth.

Was Carrie the unnatural spanner in the works psychopath, or was she the victim of one?

Chapter Nineteen

The car seemed to have a mind of its own as it pulled up outside Stan's house an hour and a half after he'd left Mandy. Ethan sat in the car and looked out at the empty street and the chinks of light behind the curtains of the home that Carrie had grown up in. It was on the cusp of being too late to just drop in on someone without an appointment, but Ethan knew that if he didn't speak to Stan he'd never get to sleep tonight. There were questions that needed answering, and this was the only place where he'd find what he needed.

His knock at the door was answered quickly as though Stan had been watching and waiting for his arrival. The man himself was dressed in trousers and a pullover and didn't look surprised to see Ethan.

"Thought you'd be back. You might as well come in, I don't want to entertain the whole street as they try and work out why you're here."

As he led Ethan down the corridor he continued, "Since all that business with Carrie everyone looks at me funny. It's always the same, blame the parents as though I somehow made her into a child killer."

Waving Ethan to one of the seats in the kitchen, Stan started filling the kettle and setting up a pair of mugs for them both. Ethan made casual chit-chat until Stan had sat down opposite him, he wanted to see his expressions when he asked his questions. This time he was here armed with more information and he was hoping he could find out a lot more. Stan, however, had his own venting to do first.

"They've got a petition you know. The families of those kids started it, and now everyone in town is signing it and sharing it online. Have you seen it?"

Ethan shook his head and watched as Stan pulled out his mobile phone and bought up the page to show him. It was one of those very emotive posts, and from the number of comments underneath, it was also proving very popular. The basic premise was that Carrie shouldn't ever be released until she admitted what she'd done and told the families where the children were. Ethan couldn't argue with it, he'd wondered himself if no matter what his report showed if Carrie would lose her parole anyway because she wouldn't talk about her crimes. The comments ranged from mildly outraged to the volatile rantings of those who spent their time online looking for reasons to spew hatred and threats. According to this, Carrie should be why the death penalty was brought back. Ethan shuddered, the thought that someone in authority played God and decided to end someone's life was abhorrent to him.

Handing the phone back to Stan he waited to see what else he'd have to say about it.

"Can't say I blame them. What she did was evil, but she's still my daughter no matter what. It ain't easy to read stuff like this, people wishing she was dead, or worse wanting to finish her off themselves like a rabid dog that needs putting down."

Ethan nodded, the words were right but there was something in the way he said them that didn't have the ring of truth about it.

"I was also hoping to talk to you about your son, Dan."

Stan's face hardened at the mention of his son, "I don't want to talk about him. He's in one of those nut houses, and that's where he'll stay."

That was a very different stance from the one he took for Carrie earlier. To Stan, it appeared that his daughter murdering three children was more forgivable than his son's mental health diagnosis.

"You can look at me like that if you want, but I'm not going to pretend that I'm not ashamed of how weak he is. Just like his mother, falls apart at the drop of a hat. I've done my share of looking after and now it's time to take care of myself."

"Has your wife ever tried to get in touch with the children?"

Ethan thought he'd asked the question casually enough, but Stan narrowed his eyes suspiciously.

"You've spoken to her, haven't you? That's why you're here, digging around because that drunken bitch has spun you a few sob stories. What was it this time? The one where I was a controlling bastard, or the one where I knocked her about? Maybe she's come up with a new one by now because god forbid that woman ever take responsibility for her own screw-ups."

He wasn't sure, but Ethan thought he could sense a touch of coldness in his words as though they were his rehearsed response. It could just be because he's irritated by the amount of times he's had to explain himself, Ethan admitted to himself. Was he looking for problems where there weren't any to be found?

"What do you think happened to those children Mr Martins?"

Stan nearly choked on his mouthful of tea as he slammed the mug on the table sloshing the brown liquid onto the surface.

"How fucking dare you. How the fuck would I know? I'm as clued up as you lot are. She went into the woods with those nippers, and they never came back out."

He got to his feet and despite Ethan being younger, fitter, and bigger, he felt intimidated by the aura of rage coming from Stan. His face was a mask of disgust and anger, and his clenched fists made Ethan wonder how close to physical violence he was. It felt as though one more wrong word would push Stan over the line, and suddenly he was desperate to get away before he escalated.

"Get out of my house. And don't bother trying to come back either."

Ethan snatched up his bag and with a hasty goodbye left the house. It didn't feel safe to outstay his welcome, but Stan hadn't quite finished with him yet. Moving in front of Ethan for a moment and blocking his exit, he leaned into his personal space.

"One last thing doctor. When you next see Carrie can you pass on a message for me? Nothing complicated, just say "Daddy knows best." She'll know what that means."

Ethan nodded and took the opportunity to swerve around Stan and get out of the house.

• • • ● ● ● ● • •

Carrie was wearing her confident mask today. She sat opposite Ethan and crossed her legs while looking at him with the expression of a businesswoman about to take part in a meeting.

"You're looking better Carrie, how are things going in general?"

Carrie smiled politely, "As well as they can be when you're locked up with a bunch of violent offenders."

Ethan nodded, "Do you not consider yourself to be a violent offender Carrie?"

She snorted, before rolling her eyes as though he'd asked the most stupid question she'd ever heard.

"That's a little blunt isn't it doctor? I thought we were working our way towards the reason why I'm here, and then you go and spoil it by just jumping in like that. I thought you were way more subtle."

Ethan had to give her points for how cleverly evasive she'd been in her reply. Deciding that it was time to take the gloves off and see how she responded to some pressure he told her he'd been to see her dad. Carrie looked irritated, but she shrugged as though she didn't care.

"I'm sure he had a lot to say, he usually does."

Ethan pulled out his notebook as though checking for what he was about to say next, but really there was no need as the message Stan had given him was unforgettable.

"He had a message for you. "Daddy knows best." What does that mean Carrie?"

She paled and dropped her head, the confident mask was gone, and in its place was a trembling, frightened child. Whatever Stan had intended with that message he'd definitely got his money's worth. Carrie looked as though she was about to throw up.

"I want to go back to my cell."

Her voice was small and quiet and she wouldn't meet his eye.

"We still have half an hour of our session to go yet Carrie. I'd rather we finish up before you leave. Why did those words upset you so much?"

Carrie shook her head and refused to answer or look at him. She darted glances at the door as though hoping the guards would come in and take her away.

"Please let me leave. I don't want to talk about it."

Ethan was tempted to let her go but this was the most honest reaction he'd had from her so far and he wanted to see where it led.

"No Carrie, you need to stay and tell me what this is about. I need you to tell me the truth."

Her reaction took him by surprise, the scared, timid child was now replaced by an angry harridan who flew out of her seat and launched herself at him. She'd hooked her fingers into claws and was trying to scratch at his face when the guards burst in and pulled her away. Carrie fought them as she continued to try to get at Ethan for another go.

"You bastard! Leave me alone. You don't know what you're asking me to do."

Carrie spat the words at him as Croft tightened her grip and yanked the smaller woman out of the room. Ethan could still hear her screaming and spitting out threats all the way down the corridor. Leaning back in his chair while he waited for his heart to stop racing he considered her extreme reaction to the message her father had passed on. Stan must've known it would have an impact, the question was, what lay behind it?

Chapter Twenty

Rachel and May were in the office when he arrived at Robin Wing. It didn't take much to work out who they wanted to discuss either.

"Carrie Martins has completely withdrawn. She refuses to leave her cell, she isn't eating meals with the others, and she won't talk to any of us."

The information that May was handing over didn't come as a surprise to Ethan. Considering their last meeting and her reaction to the message from her father, he'd been expecting some additional fallout. He'd watched the video back earlier in his office to see if he could see any warning signs that she was going to blow. He'd ended up pausing it on the image of her launching herself at him. Her teeth barred like an attack dog, her eyes narrow slits of rage as she'd acted on pure instinct. Was this the real Carrie? Had she always been prone to fits of violent anger and just been good at hiding it? He could see that Rachel and May were still waiting for him to answer so pulled himself back into the room.

"I'm not sure that she'll talk to me either. We didn't part on particularly good terms last time, I'm sure you've seen the incident report already."

Rachel shrugged, "We need to at least try. We've not had a violent incident with her before, her usual behaviour is to get others to do her dirty work. You apparently got under her skin enough to provoke that response so we're hoping you might get through to her now."

Ethan gave a wry grin, "So I'm bait? I'll just hope you guys are quick enough to get to her before she scratches my eyes out shall I?"

May and Rachel chuckled and May added, "No one's going to let it get that far, you'll be fine. Rachel, can you do the honours?"

Rachel nodded, "Although she can be a sour-faced whatsit it's a shame Croft's off today, she'd have been useful if it all kicks off."

Carrie's room was across the corridor from the office. Rachel knocked and then pushed the door open so Ethan could go inside. The curtains were drawn and the lights were dimmed. It took a moment to acclimatise to the gloom and see the hump under the bedclothes. Carrie didn't so much as move, but Ethan got the impression she was awake and alert to who'd come in.

"Carrie, I know I'm probably the last person you want to see right now but the staff are worried about you."

Nothing.

The silence drew out until it filled the room like an uncomfortable aura swirling between them. Ethan remained by the door where he could leave in a hurry if she did try to attack him again, but he was pretty sure she wouldn't. The rage she'd thrown at him seemed to have receded into a dark depression – or was this yet another mask that Carrie had thrown on to deceive him? How better to avoid having to talk to him about her offence than to put up a wall to block him out.

"Can you tell me what it was about your dad's message that upset you so much?"

A sniff from under the covers suggested Carrie was crying but she didn't reply. Ethan leaned against the doorframe, he wasn't sure what more he could try. It was also possible that this was the end of their professional relationship, and Ethan was surprised at how disappointed he felt at that idea. It wasn't just that he hadn't got to the bottom of who Carrie really was, although that was a big part of it, he'd also wanted to solve the mystery of what really happened to those children.

"Carrie, I'm going to leave now because I think my being here is upsetting you more. If you decide you'd like to talk to me let one of the staff know and they'll pass it on to me. I'd very much like us to continue working together, but I understand if that's not what you want."

Another sniff, this time louder, and then a small voice muffled by the blankets came from the bed.

"I'd like to keep working with you, Dr Quinn."

It was a breakthrough of sorts and Ethan tried to capitalise on it, "You really need to try and eat please Carrie. I'll see you on Monday for our usual appointment though."

The blankets moved as Carrie nodded her head and Ethan decided it was a good place to leave things. Rachel and May were hovering in the corridor and both gave him a questioning look when he approached them.

"She's said she'll continue working with me and I've prompted her to start eating again. She didn't have a lot to say in response but I'm hopeful she took it in."

The whole situation had left Ethan feeling emotionally drained, and he was pleased to get back to his office where he threw himself into his other cases. The rest of Friday flew by in a blur of calls, emails, and one-to-one sessions. Ethan was just packing up his things and locking his desk when his phone rang. It was Cal and he sounded full of news.

"I've got another contact for us. A lady who says her older sister was friends with Carrie at school. She's got a story for us but didn't want to get into it over the phone."

Ethan paused, it was starting to feel intrusive how far he was digging into Carrie's past, but at the same time, he was also desperate for answers. Cal seemed to pick up on his hesitation.

"Her name's Selina Winters. She's kept this story to herself but the idea that Carrie might be released frightened her enough that she felt it needed sharing. She's legit Doc, totally legit. I haven't offered her money or any sort of reward, she's genuinely doing this because she feels her story needs telling."

Ethan tapped his pen on the notebook next to his computer, it did sound intriguing and he'd like to know the Carrie that the other children had seen growing up. You could learn a lot from childhood behaviours, he thought as he agreed to go along and arranged to meet Cal the next morning.

Selina Winters must've been waiting behind the front door because she opened it before they'd even got close enough to ring her doorbell.

"I'm still not sure I should be doing this. What if she gets out and hears that I've been talking about her? What's stopping her coming for me?"

Ethan gave her a reassuring smile as he introduced himself.

"I'm Dr Quinn, I completely understand your reticence. If, and it's a big if, Carrie does get released she'll be issued with a new identity far away from the area where her crimes were committed."

Selina appeared mollified and stepped back to let them in. Her house was small and cluttered, dust motes danced across the surfaces and the aroma of fried food hung in the air. Selina was a short woman with the pasty skin of someone who didn't get out much. When her offer of a hot drink was refused she led them into the kitchen where she set about making herself one while she talked.

"I'm going to get this off my chest quickly because if I don't I think I'll chicken out and it'll stay unsaid. Carrie hung around with my older sister, Angela, for a while when she first started secondary school. It was a short-lived acquaintance, I hesitate to call them friends as it didn't last that long. Angela found moving up to big school difficult and struggled to make friends and it always felt like Carrie read that on her and moved in. Anyway, they hung about most evenings after school and on weekends. I'd often ask to go out with them but they'd tell me I was too little. Angela hadn't been like that before, I think it was Carrie's influence but my mum put it down to her age. Mum wasn't that keen on their friendship, she thought Carrie was a bad influence because Angela started to get into all sorts of trouble. at school. They both made fun of me and a couple of times Carrie made me cry. Once I spilled some juice on one of her notebooks and she grabbed me by the arm and shook me until I cried.

It didn't stop me wanting to go places with them, but they never let me. That's why it was such a surprise when they invited me to go with them to make a den in the abandoned building site near the park. It was all fenced off but some of the bigger boys had cut a hole so they could sneak in and drink beers and smoke where the grown-ups wouldn't catch them. Carrie and Angela planned to use that as a way to get in and then set up a little den. I couldn't believe they wanted me along too. I remember bouncing along next to them full of excitement that I was being included. They were both so nice as well, talking about how the three of us would have a special place that no one else knew about. It wasn't until we got there that the whole atmosphere changed. We were stood looking down through the broken floorboards and Angela commented on how far the drop was. I leaned over to look and as I did Carrie grabbed my arms. At first, I thought she was holding on to keep me safe, but when they both started laughing I realised it wasn't."

Selina drew in a shaky breath, it was as though she was that frightened child again.

"She lifted me up and the next thing I knew my feet were dangling over the hole. I closed my eyes so I couldn't see how far I'd fall if she let me go. I was hoping Angela might step in and put a stop to it but she just stood by and let it happen.

"What if I drop you?"

To me, Carrie sounded thoughtful as though considering it as an option.

"I think you'd land with a big splat on the ground. You'd be spread all over the floor like a squashed blackberry. There'd be blood everywhere."

I was crying and begging her to pull me back in by then, but that just seemed to egg her on. Eventually, my screams must've got to Angie because she grabbed me around the waist and yanked me toward her. Carrie had a face like thunder, I could see she was really pissed that Angela had stopped her fun. As soon as my feet touched safe ground I ran as fast as I could and I didn't stop running until I got home. Angela wasn't far behind me and she told Mum why I was crying so hard I couldn't speak for myself. I've never seen my mum so angry, not with us, but with Carrie. She picked up her bag and told us to stay put and stormed out of the house. We followed her anyway and hid behind the hedge at Carrie's house while Mum banged on the door and yelled at her dad. He didn't seem at all bothered. He laughed in Mum's face and told her she was overreacting to what sounded like a children's game. Then he just slammed the front door in Mum's face."

Selina wiped her eyes on her sleeve and gave a big sniff, and for a moment Ethan could imagine what she'd have looked like as a small child.

"Mum wouldn't let us play with her anymore but we wouldn't have done anyway. Her little brother was alright, quiet, and a bit strange but not like her."

This was a damning story of Carrie's past behaviour if taken at face value, but was it just the boundary-pushing of an adolescent that was growing up without a mother and a father who struggled to show affection?

Chapter Twenty-One

The call from Dr Alexander had come out of the blue.

"Sorry to bother you at a weekend Dr Quinn but I was hoping you'd come to visit Dan again. Since your last visit I'd describe him as more unsettled, but not in an entirely negative way. He's definitely more engaged with his surroundings and more responsive. It might be a coincidence but I can't help but think it's linked to you."

Ethan quickly agreed to go out to the hospital. He couldn't help but wonder if Dan was getting to a point where he might be more capable of sharing whatever it was that had gone on in that house while the two of them were growing up.

Stella was waiting for him in reception when he arrived, and she filled him in as they took the lift up to the ward.

"Dan has been less inclined to just sit and draw, he's been pacing his room and muttering to himself. We haven't been able to pick anything out but he gets quite animated which isn't like him at all. He's been here since he was sixteen years old and at first, he was almost catatonic. We saw the drawing as an improvement and assumed that the violent images were a result of what his sister did to those poor children. He's taken a lot of his artwork off the walls and stacked them neatly on his desk, and what's left is almost a timeline of a story. We've tried, but we can't work out what he's trying to tell us and hoped that with your more intimate knowledge of his sister, you might understand it."

Considering he still couldn't always work out if Carrie was lying or not that was a bit of a stretch but Ethan nodded anyway as he was eager to get to Dan's room. If he'd been expecting a miraculous change then he was on a hiding to being disappointed. Dan was hunched over a sheet of paper on his desk his face scrunched up in concentration as he scribbled furiously with coloured pencils. Ethan greeted him, and even though Dan didn't look around to acknowledge his presence he got the impression that he was very aware of him. Taking in the walls he was surprised to see that the layers of drawings were indeed replaced by a few chosen ones. They were no longer haphazard. As Stella had said, they were now in a perfect line around the wall. It was hard to know where it started, or even if there was a starting point at all. The red shoe had pride of place above his bed and the others consisted of stick figures of various shapes and sizes and horrific faces that he'd coloured red. Ethan had done a little work on interpreting art and these images suggested rage, despair, and possibly fear.

Looking at Dan he noticed he'd stopped his frantic drawing and instead was clutching a wad of paper. When he caught Ethan's eye he held them out for him to take. They were all along the same theme. Circles in red with wide mouths and angry eyes, and stick figures cowering from another larger figure. To Ethan, this could be interpreted in two ways. Either the bigger figure was his father or it was someone who may not be physically larger in real life and instead was given that appearance because of their impact on Dan.

Although they spoke to him as a description of Dan's internal angst, Ethan was finding it hard to work out what he was trying to tell him with them. There was a look on Dan's face that suggested he was expecting Ethan to solve the mystery of what his pictures meant, and it frustrated Ethan that he couldn't understand them. Some were obvious or appeared that way to Ethan. Little stick figures dancing around lollypop trees suggested this particular one was Dan's depiction of what his sister had done. Another seemed to show the little red shoe that was all that was found of Tessie Conner. This seemed to be a recurring theme and one that Dan drew over and over again.

Ethan took the spare seat next to Dan so they sat side by side. He'd often found with the more paranoid, anxious patients that when they weren't forced to make face-to-face contact they were more inclined to speak to him.

"Dan, I saw your mother. She was very worried about you and she's hoping to come and visit. She hasn't been well herself but she feels strong enough to see you now."

He kept his words simple, almost as though speaking to a child. At first, he thought that Dan hadn't taken anything in but then he saw a lone tear roll down his cheek. They sat in silence for a while, Ethan hoping that Dan would take comfort from his presence and that he may feel able to say something. Dan, however, didn't say a word. When Stella returned she took in the stack of drawings Ethan was holding.

"Now that is a privilege. Dan doesn't usually let them out of his sight."

Ethan understood the significance of Dan reaching out, but what he didn't get was why now? Had Ethan's presence in his life triggered Dan to start engaging, and was it because he had a story he wanted to tell?

· · ● · ● · ● ● · ·

Carrie's left eye was almost completely swollen closed. There were also smaller bruises on her face and what looked like fingertip bruising on her left arm. When he gave a shocked gasp at her appearance she shrugged before answering him.

"As you can see I'm as popular as ever."

Ethan frowned, "Do the staff know you were assaulted again? Who was it?"

Carrie let out a cold burst of laughter, "As if I'm going to be stupid enough to name names ever again. I learned my lesson last time."

As far as Ethan knew she hadn't told anyone who'd assaulted her last time, but maybe she meant the staff's reaction. They hadn't exactly been sympathetic and maybe she felt it wasn't worth making trouble for herself if no one would believe her anyway.

"This is a serious assault, Carrie, your eye looks terrible. Has anyone checked you over?"

"They offered but I told them not to bother. It'll heal, and besides, should I really care if it doesn't? I'm spending the rest of my life here with women who loathe me, if everyone thinks I'm a monster maybe it's better I look the part."

Ethan wasn't sure if she was seeking sympathy, or if she was just stating the facts as she saw them.

"We need to continue to work on our sessions Carrie. Your best chance of getting parole is to be honest and forthcoming about your offence. You'll be asked about your guilt and they look more positively on those who can admit to it."

Carrie looked at him coldly through her one good eye, "Maybe I'm not guilty, ever thought about that doctor?"

That was the sum total of the information he got out of her that session. She clearly hadn't forgiven him for passing on her dad's message because she point-blank refused to take part in telling him any-thing else about her past. When he followed her back to the wing he approached Rachel and asked her about Carrie's injuries.

"We think it's most likely she did it to herself. Did you see how they were all on her left side when she's right-handed? She's watched more closely than usual and we'd have noticed if anyone had attacked her. Besides, she won't tell us who, and without that there isn't much we can do about it."

Ethan was a little taken aback by her attitude to what looked like either a serious assault or a very nasty self-harm incident. He also wasn't sure how to raise his concerns. Falling out with the staff wasn't a great move, but he knew he couldn't ignore it either. He decided it was probably time to take this to his mentor. They were supposed to have had a one-to-one by now but Dr Edwards had been on leave for a while and had only been back a couple of days.

As it turned out Dr Edwards was also eager to see him and asked him to come straight over for a chat. Ethan glanced at the clock, it wasn't long until his day finished, but he wanted to get this conversa-tion out of the way.

Chapter Twenty-Two

D r Edwards shuffled the papers on his desk before clicking the top of his biro a few times.

"I've heard your concerns Ethan, but I also need to pass on the feedback I've had from Robin Wing. They feel you're too close to Carrie Martins and you're not objective enough about her. Some staff have gone so far as to claim you take her side against theirs."

Ethan felt a slow burn of annoyance, "That's unfair and untrue. I have a duty to report anything relevant she says to the staff team and what they do with it is then up to them. It would be unsafe, unprofessional, and above all unethical, to assume that everything she says is a lie and to ignore it."

Dr Edwards looked uncomfortable at his position as piggie in the middle.

"I agree Ethan, of course I do, but we need to look at maintaining safe boundaries and keeping a professional distance. With that out of the way, can you fill me in on how your report is coming along? The parole board has been in touch to ask as they need to schedule a date."

"It's coming along Jim, I'm hopeful that I'll have something close to a conclusion for you in the next few weeks."

Dr Edwards sighed and clicked his pen again, "We were hopeful you'd have or be very close to a conclusion by now Ethan. Taking into account the potential risk to the community as well as the cost of providing Martins with a new identity and new life.."

He tailed off for a moment as he waited to see if Ethan got the point he was making.

"Are you suggesting that the expectation is for a negative outcome?"

Jim looked awkward at being asked so directly, "Of course not. The outcome was never, and should never be, pre-determined. All I'm saying is that you need to be aware of those considerations when you write the final report."

Well worded, thought Ethan, it was obvious what he meant but he'd managed to sugarcoat it so Ethan couldn't complain he was being pushed in any one particular direction.

"I think the best thing to do is for you to give me a weekly update, that way I can reassure the powers that be that everything is in hand."

Ethan was pretty sure that decision had already been made and that Jim had decided to slip it in as though it was something he'd just come up with. The rest of their one-to-one focused on Ethan's other patients and general well-being questions. Apart from Carrie, he was making slow but steady progress with his caseload and Dr Edwards commended him for how he'd managed some of the transfers to more appropriate settings.

"It's incredibly challenging to access secure beds in the community and I know you must feel frustrated, but you've already achieved some excellent results."

Frustration was an understatement, thought Ethan. Mental health resources were already decimated, and the people on his caseload were often a low priority. He tried to stay out of politics, in his experience no matter who was in charge mental health came at the bottom of the health funding list. The problem was that he could no longer ignore how much worse it was now. Ethan was an advocate for prevention rather than the firefighting they were currently engaged in. With the right level of support and treatment, most people would be able to manage in the community. Yet due to the lack of staff and resources, this wasn't happening. As a result, many people became so unwell they needed access to the few psychiatric beds available.

There was no point dwelling on it. Ethan found that the longer he worked in mental health the more upsetting it was that the most vulnerable were often disregarded. Dr Edwards was of a similar opinion and both men took the opportunity to vent their feelings. This meant that their meeting was left on a more positive note of mutual agreement, and Ethan felt less demoralised than he had earlier. He was still annoyed about how the staff on Robin Wing had been talking about him behind his back, but at least he felt as though he could see them without feeling the need to raise it. There was no point harbouring ill will against the staff, it would strain his working relationship with them and that would be counterproductive when it came to doing the best he could for his patients.

Dr Edwards, clearly pleased to have got the whole situation dealt with pointed at the clock.

"Time you were getting off. Thank you for staying late today and hopefully we can just put this to bed now."

Ethan nodded and bid his boss good night before leaving. All the way home he mulled it over in his head until he eventually came to the conclusion that it was best left unmentioned when he saw the staff the next morning. Letting himself into his house he realised he hadn't remembered to leave the small lamp on in the hall. As a result, it was pitch black and he swore as he tripped on a small box that contained his shoes. He really needed to unpack and start putting his house together. Ethan knew deep down he was avoiding settling because he was still grieving for his lost marriage and the home they'd shared. It wasn't so much Andrea that he missed, it was more coming back to someone. He was a man happy with his own company most of the time, but he was aware that he was becoming isolated and lonely.

He was too tired tonight to do too much, but after putting on some background music he did manage to unpack a couple of boxes of books. With the shelves looking more full the living room suddenly felt a little more homely. Keeping himself occupied had also kept his mind off of Carrie. Did the staff have a point, was he becoming too obsessed with her case? She was a puzzle to be solved, and he was increasingly finding himself unable to walk away from getting answers.

Ethan had noticed some of the staff looked uncomfortable when he first walked in the next day, but once they realised that he wasn't planning to raise their complaints the atmosphere thawed slightly. It wasn't that he didn't still feel aggrieved, it was more that he'd decided there was nothing to be gained from making a point of it. Focusing on some of his other caseload he was pleased to hear that the woman he'd been working with on her anxiety had made some small but significant improvements.

"Lauren seems a lot less stressed and has even managed some time out in the communal areas. She still has a tendency to isolate herself from the others, but she looks more relaxed in their company."

Rachel seemed pleased to hand over this piece of positive news, and it reminded him how invested the staff were in the prisoner's recovery. Robin Wing was less of a custodial environment and more about care and support. It wasn't until they were alone in the office that she raised the elephant in the room.

"I wasn't part of the delegation who went to Dr Edwards about you and Carrie Martins. I just wanted you to know that as far as I'm concerned I'd raise any issues with you directly rather than going behind your back. I don't want this to sit between us when we have to work so closely with each other."

Ethan appreciated her comments and it went a long way to making him feel that the entire staff team wasn't against him. It did make him wonder who'd been the instigator, but he didn't have to wait long to find out. Back in his office and working through the mountain of paperwork in front of him he'd been interrupted by May.

"Dr Quinn, if I may have a moment of your time?"

Ethan nodded, with May being so formal in her approach to him he was pretty sure she was about to address the complaints made to his line manager.

"I wanted to talk to you about the Carrie Martin's case. I'm sure Dr Edwards has raised our concerns with you and I felt I should be upfront that I was the one who went to him."

Ethan was momentarily unsure what to say. What do you say to a colleague who you feel has breached the unspoken trust you should have between you?

"Thank you for coming to me about it May. I appreciate that you've been open about this with me, but I also feel that it would've been helpful to hear it from you before involving Dr Edwards."

May coloured slightly at the mild rebuke, "It's not exactly the easiest thing to bring up. I just feel that you've become sucked into her manipulative little world and I don't want that to affect your report."

Warming to her theme she became more impassioned, "If someone as dangerous as the Child Catcher gets released then everyone is at risk. It's clear she isn't anywhere near rehabilitated and that means she shouldn't be let out."

Ethan felt a little uncomfortable with her use of Carrie's sensationalist nickname that the media had foisted on her but felt it wouldn't be helpful to pull her up about it. He was a bit surprised too. While she'd always been negative about her, he hadn't noticed that she had any strong feelings, but suddenly she seemed very opinionated.

"I'm not going to be taking any chances May. I'm well aware of what the risks are and that Carrie shouldn't be taken at face value. All I'm trying to do is to build a relationship with her where she might be more honest than she has been previously."

May seemed reassured by this and nodded her agreement. She seemed a little warmer when she left and Ethan hoped things were cleared up between them. Suddenly the office felt claustrophobic and Ethan had an urge to get out and breathe some fresh air. It felt as though everyone around him wasn't who he'd thought.

Chapter Twenty-Three

The call from Stella came through when he was halfway home. Pulling the car over into a layby he'd barely had a chance to greet her when she launched into the reason she was ringing.

"Dan's gone. He's absconded from the unit and we've got no idea where he is. He's never done this before, he's had no interest in the outside world until you came along."

This was said with a sting of bitterness and Ethan got the impression that he was climbing up her shitty list.

"When did you notice him gone?"

Stella took a deep breath, "Just after lunch. He didn't show up to collect his food so one of the staff took it to him. His bed was neatly made and his drawing things were missing. He must've packed them up and taken them with him. We've called the police, but a missing patient is rarely a priority for them."

Ethan's mind raced through the little he knew about Dan as he tried to think where he might have gone.

"I'll start looking for him and call you if I find him."

Stella was still chilly as she thanked him and hung up, clearly she felt this was all his fault for some reason. There wasn't time to think about it now, a vulnerable young man was god knows where and he had to try and think of the most likely places to try. Dan's pictures were on his mobile phone from when he'd photographed them. Ethan scrolled through until he found them, and then enlarging them as much as the screen allowed, he flicked through trying to work out the locations.

There was what Ethan believed to be his family home, and he didn't think he'd head there. Stan didn't appear to be the sort of father that Dan would seek out in his time of need. There were also a lot of buildings that Ethan didn't recognise and a few that he did. The school, the library, and one that looked like a building site. Was that the one where Carrie had dangled her friend's sister over a hole all those years ago? If so it suggested that Dan had known about it. Had he watched the drama unfold, and had it added to his mental health decline?

The darkest of the pictures was of a group of trees. Their arm-like branches creeping across the page creating a canopy above the small stick people below. To Ethan, this looked like the woods where Carrie had taken those children for their last walk. He shuddered, did he really want to go searching through the woods for a young man who'd absconded from a secure hospital? The sensible voice was shoved rudely aside by the one who always demanded answers. Ethan wasn't someone who could just turn their back on a mystery like this. Deep down he knew he'd got himself in too deep, but it was far too late to walk away.

Turning the car around he headed toward Worthingford, his mind ticking over with ideas of where to start. Remembering how Mrs. Mayhew had described Dan's enjoyment of the library he decided he may as well give that a go first. It was virtually empty, ignoring the questioning look of the librarian he speed walked around the shelves and tables double-checking. The only customers were an old man with his flat cap pulled down low over his face to hide the fact he was snoozing rather than reading, and a serious-looking young woman in the non-fiction section. Barely pausing on his way out he worked out where the old building site would've been. As he'd thought it was no longer a half-finished adventure playground for the local kids. Instead, it was now a swanky block of flats complete with balconies and perfectly maintained gardens. Just in case Dan had found his way here Ethan did a circuit of the building, but he was nowhere to be seen. Considering there was little likelihood of him seeking out his father there was only one more place to try.

Ringwald Woods.

Ethan hesitated at the point where the path curved into the woods. There was something sinister about how the trees bent down towards him their branches knitting together as though they were one. It was still daylight but inside the woods, it was gloomy and dark. Ethan was tempted to walk away, but telling himself he was being stupid he forced himself to go in.

He had no idea where he was going but decided that sticking to the path was a good place to start. At least that way he could easily find his way back out again. It was a fairly easy walk, the path was flat and if he hadn't known the dark past of the area he'd have enjoyed the peacefulness. There was no sign of Dan, and Ethan was starting to wonder if this was going to be another dead end. If it was, he was all out of ideas and Dan would have to stay missing until the police got around to finding him.

Rounding a corner Ethan stopped in his tracks. There wasn't anything else ahead of him apart from more path and the sparkle of the sunlight where the trees opened back out much further away. Standing still and looking around him he noticed there was a patch of ground where the nettles and leaves had been flattened. Impulsively following it he stumbled down the gentle embankment until he reached a small clearing at the bottom. A large oak tree took up most of the space, and behind it, he could see another embankment. This one looked as though it had a sheer drop. Ethan carefully shuffled the rest of the way down to where he could see a small figure huddled next to the tree. Dan's arms were wrapped around the thick trunk, and a small rucksack was tucked between his knees. His head was resting on the bark and he was so still Ethan couldn't even tell if he was breathing until he got closer.

"Dan, it's Dr Quinn. Are you okay?"

The young man barely moved, but Ethan was sure he saw his eyes flicker sideways.

"You must be cold there Dan. I've got a blanket in the car, shall we go and fetch it for you?"

By now Ethan had managed to get close enough to Dan that he was able to tap his arm gently to prompt him to move. The young man flinched and gripped the tree tighter so Ethan crouched down next to him.

"Dan, it's okay, I don't mean you any harm. We need to get back to the hospital, everyone is really worried about you."

The young man slowly let go of the trunk and eased himself onto his feet. Without so much as a glance at Ethan, he stroked the tree thoughtfully one last time, and then headed off in the direction of the path. Ethan followed him, his mind racing with questions.

Carrie had thawed slightly, she wasn't overly friendly, but she did seem willing to take part in their sessions again. Ethan let her settle in with a bit of light conversation about how she was before bringing up her brother.

"Dan absconded from the hospital last night, I found him in the woods clinging to a big Oak tree. What do you think is the significance of that spot for him?"

There was a flash of fear that passed across her face so fast he wondered if he'd imagined it. She shrugged before answering and kept her tone casually disinterested.

"Who knows? He's been locked away in a nut house for so long anything could be going on in his head. I don't know why you insist on putting so much significance on what he says or does."

Ethan had to admit there was a ring of truth to what she'd said. Was he overreading the behaviour of a vulnerable man with a significant mental health diagnosis?

"From what I could gather from the reports I read from the time of the murders, that particular tree he chose isn't far from where the police found Tessie Conner's shoe."

Carrie narrowed her eyes and gave another deep sigh as though irritated by the direction his conversation was taking.

"Coincidence I imagine. That or he's created a delusion around it all. Anyway, enough of Dan and his madness, what did you want me to talk about today?"

It was noticeable how swiftly Carrie had bought it back to herself. Either she was the narcissistic psychopath the system had labeled her, or she was trying to avoid him looking too deeply at Dan's actions. It was hard to tell with Carrie, so Ethan decided the best bet was to move forward with her own story. They were getting closer to the murders and he wanted to ease her into the idea that eventually she'd need to talk about it.

"Let's talk about when you started your job as a teaching assistant. You'd just left the library at this point."

Carrie looked relieved to be moving on from the topic of Dan even though it meant moving onto a part of her own story that she'd been reluctant to address.

Chapter Twenty-Four

Carrie

It was exciting, but scary at the same time.

Becoming a teaching assistant felt as though it was one step closer to me reaching my dream job of being a teacher. On my first day, I spent ages getting ready. I must've gone through nearly every outfit in my wardrobe trying to pick something smart and appropriate. My dad was no help, he scorned my efforts and told me I was wasting my time.

"You're a nobody Carrie, a lowly teaching assistant that they'll shove out the door as soon as the budgets get tight. You'd have been better off staying at the library."

It was hard to maintain my enthusiasm with him putting a dampener on things, but as I looked in the mirror I told myself I looked the part. The first day was awkward at first, I didn't know where I was supposed to be, and that made me late to the classroom. I'd been allocated Class 4, where the seven-year-olds were and the teacher was Monica Hayes. I'd seen her and spoken to her a few times at the library and she'd seemed really nice, but that first morning it was obvious she wasn't pleased with me.

I don't know why, but I did hear that a friend of her's applied for the post so maybe she was upset that I got the job. Whatever it was she made it clear from day one that I was someone that she had to tolerate and no more. It made working with her really hard. Even the kids picked up on it and used to ask me what was wrong with Miss Hayes, and "Why doesn't Miss Hayes like you?"

I had no idea how to answer that so I'd just pretend they were imagining things. One day it was so bad that I had to sneak off for a cry. Monica had been difficult and snappy with me all day and when she whispered in my ear that I was useless I almost burst into tears in front of the class. I excused myself so I could leave the room, and I ended up hiding in the toilets until I heard the bell sound for break time. I was about to wash my face and hide the tears when the door opened and two of the pupils from my class came in.

Tessie and Emily were inseparable, best friends who held hands and always sat together. They asked me what was wrong so of course I lied and said I had a tummy ache. Neither girl believed me.

"I saw Miss Hayes talking to you, did she make you cry?"

I shook my head and repeated the story about my tummy ache before excusing myself so I didn't have to lie to them anymore. By then I really did feel ill so I went to reception and told them I had to go home. I stayed off for the rest of that week, but when I went back on Monday there was even more of an atmosphere in the classroom.

I didn't find out what Monica was annoyed with me about until she confronted me in the staff room claiming I'd told the girls that she'd upset me.

"You're trying to drive a wedge between me and the pupils and I won't stand for it. I've spoken to the head and I want you out of my classroom. Someone else can take you on, but I don't want you there anymore."

I was so frightened, if she pushed me out and they didn't have anywhere else for me then would the head end my probation? I'd heard the library had already replaced me so if they did I'd be out of a job. I knew the girls were just sticking up for me but that wasn't what I'd told them at all. I had no idea why they were lying all I knew was that it had got me into a lot of trouble. Monica must've told the other staff about it before I got there because they were all staring at me. I'd just made myself a mug of tea, but I couldn't face drinking it so I poured it down the sink and left the room. I spent the whole break wandering the school grounds until it was time to go back to work.

The rest of the day was miserable. I did my job as best I could but Tessie and Emily kept asking if I was okay. I told them I was fine and my tummy ache was better now and hoped they'd leave it at that. I tried to remember they were just little kids who thought they were looking out for me, but I think I was probably a bit short with them. Every time I spoke to them Monica glared at me and it was just horrible and uncomfortable. The only time she smiled was when she passed me the note that told me to go see the head before going home. It was more of a smug smirk and I knew it meant he was going to be telling me off.

Mr Hardcastle, the head of the school, was usually a smiley man who I felt comfortable with. Today he looked as stern as if I was a naughty child who'd set off the fire alarms.

"I've had some concerns raised that you aren't managing your role to the level we'd expect by this point in your probation. I'm sure I don't need to remind you that if you don't pass your evaluations we may need to end your employment."

This was my worst fear, that I'd be kicked out of my job just because Monica had taken against me. My eyes filled with tears, I knew it was no good telling him what was really happening because it would just look as though I was making excuses. I managed to say I was sorry and that I'd try harder, and he patted my shoulder and assured me that we all wanted this to work I just needed to do better.

All the way home I felt sick to my stomach. I didn't know what to do, if I couldn't fix things with Monica then eventually she'd get her way and I'd be fired. All evening I couldn't think of anything else, and it wasn't long before my dad noticed how distracted I was. I played it down and just told him that two of the girls in my class had been making up stories and that the teacher wasn't happy with me. I couldn't sleep and I must've looked like crap when I showed up the next day.

Monica barely even nodded a hello to me and when the bell went for break she told me to stay behind. I wondered if maybe she wanted to clear the air between us, but that couldn't have been further from the truth.

"Someone keyed my car last night Carrie. They also poured paint stripper on the boot. It's a lot of damage and it feels very odd that this would happen after the head addressed the probation issues with you. Did you go to my house last night and damage my car?"

I shook my head, this was really bad. If she thought I'd damaged her car there was no chance she'd ever get off my case. Worse than that she might go to the police and I had a good idea who'd really done it. It was just the kind of thing my dad liked to do when someone upset one of us. I remembered how I'd heard the front door open and close in the early hours of the morning. Had he sneaked over to Monica's house and trashed her car?

"I hope this wasn't you Carrie. I've reported it to the police and they'll be looking for evidence. If you did it, they'll pick you up for it."

She turned her face away from me making sure I knew I was dismissed. I trailed miserably out of the room and the rest of the day was awful. When I got home I mentioned it to Dad, and when he smiled I knew it was him even though he didn't say so outright.

"Well, that's a pity, isn't it? Couldn't happen to a nicer person though. Looks like your Miss Hayes has upset the wrong person doesn't it?"

I didn't raise it with my dad again, and I never found out if she really did call the police. All I know is that no one came to speak to me about it.

After that, there seemed to be an unspoken truce in the classroom. We settled into a kind of routine of tolerating each other and keeping our opinions to ourselves. I guess looking back, it was more me that kept quiet. I found that if I did as I was told and didn't try to make any suggestions things went fine. I wasn't happy, and there were times I wished that I'd just stayed at the library, but I tried to focus on what I wanted from the future. This was supposed to be my gateway into being a teacher, and I was determined to achieve my goal despite Miss Hayes trying to stop me.

Chapter Twenty-Five

Carrie had fallen silent after that, and no matter how Ethan prompted she wouldn't continue. They were drawing near to the main event, and Carrie was more reluctant than ever to move on in her story. Ethan could see she was drained from what she'd already shared and decided to call it a day. Carrie thanked him quietly and looked very subdued as the guards led her back to the wing. It was hard because Ethan wanted to believe her. It wasn't nice to think a patient was lying to him constantly, but he knew from past experience that taking Carrie at face value wasn't enough either.

The rest of the day passed quickly. One of his other patients had a crisis and he spent much of the afternoon trying to find her a bed in a secure hospital. Strangely his Carrie research paid off when he tried Stella to see if there was space at her facility. It was a long shot, especially if she was still as annoyed with him as she'd seemed the last time they spoke. He needn't of worried, Stella sounded upbeat and the first thing she did was to apologise for not calling him to thank him for finding Dan sooner.

"I've been run off my feet, but that's no excuse for bad manners. I think I might have been a bit off with you when I called too. Nothing personal, I was just stressed at the thought of losing a vulnerable patient and feeling responsible."

Ethan told her he understood exactly how that felt, "There's nothing more worrying than a patient going AWOL Stella, not a problem. Actually, I was calling in the hopes of a favour."

"Considering I'm currently in the position of owing you one, fire away, and if it's in my power to give it's yours."

"You might regret that when I tell you what it's about! I'm looking for a high secure bed for one of the inmates at HMP Chartridge. She's had a rapid relapse and can't be managed safely here, but as you know resources are very limited and I've had no joy finding her a bed."

Stella was silent for a moment while Ethan crossed his fingers under the table.

"Actually, I can help. We moved one of our female high-secure patients down to medium yesterday. I can get her room turned around and ready by this afternoon if that's any good to you?"

Ethan could've hugged her, this was the answer to his biggest problem at the moment. Thanking her profusely he then remembered to ask how Dan was.

"You're very welcome. Dan is doing okay, better than before in fact. He's a little more responsive, and not as obsessive with his drawing. He sat and ate his food in the communal dining room this week which is a first for him. He sat on his own and didn't speak to anyone but it's a big step."

Ethan was pleased to hear Dan was starting to make progress, for a man who'd spent his whole adult life in hospital it was a huge improvement. By the time he left for the day, Ethan was starting to feel a bit more optimistic about everything. That feeling didn't last long, when he got outside he found Cal hanging around the gates waiting for him. Ethan indicated that he'd meet him at the pub they went to last time and had a quick look around to make sure that no one had spotted them talking. The last thing he needed was for anyone to link him with a journalist who was about to break a story on one of his patients.

Cal spread the files and photos across the table and picked up his pint while Ethan looked through.

"I'm putting together some background on the families of Carrie's victims. I also need a bit more history so I'm planning to head back to Worthingford and see if anyone else will talk."

Ethan flicked through the yellowed newspapers, mostly it was similar to the articles he'd read on line when he'd first been allocated, Carrie. The cruel nickname "Child Catcher" was often accompanied by a still of the character they'd named her after. A sinister man in a long black coat who tempted unwary children into a cage using sweets as the bait. Just in case the average reader couldn't work it out for themselves, the articles explained that Carrie too had tempted the children away using her role as a teaching assistant to gain their trust.

It wasn't until he reached the last articles that he spotted it. The picture jumped out of the page and hit him in the face like a punch. It had been taken during the court case and a photographer had caught the families heading into court together. The black and white shot showed them clumped together, holding hands and with stunned faces that tried to make sense of the chaos they'd found themselves in. The face that had given him the shock was at the front. She was turned toward the camera and it had caught her full frontal giving him a clear enough view to identify her. She hadn't changed much over the last fifteen years, older and more worn, but it was definitely May Chambers.

May glared at him, clearly angry that he'd found out her secret. She didn't look especially sorry that she'd lied to him either.

"So what? Yes, I'm Emily Little's sister. I got married and changed my name to Chambers, no mystery there. Why should I go around telling everyone my private business?"

That didn't cut any ice with Ethan, "May, that's not going to help. You're working with the woman who was convicted of killing your little sister. Surely you can see that's a complete breach of the regulations. Let alone that there's no way you can be objective about her."

May scowled at him, "And I guess you're planning to run to Dr Edwards and pay me back for what I said about you? It's not as though you're the poster child for perfection is it? Who was that man you met yesterday after work? Was it him who told you who I was?"

Ethan hid a sigh, so someone had been watching him when he left. He waved a hand at her, trying to calm the situation.

"I'm not that petty May, and I'm insulted you'd think so."

Crossing his fingers superstitiously behind his back he added, "And I don't know what you're trying to insinuate, but that was an old friend meeting me for a drink. I do think that you should tell Jim yourself though. If I found out, someone else will, and it'll be worse if you haven't got in there first."

May collapsed into the chair opposite. With all the fight drained out of her she looked exhausted. She ran a tired hand through the hair and then polished her glasses before pushing them back on her nose.

"You don't know what it was like Ethan. The press were like vultures picking our grief clean. They wouldn't leave us alone, if anyone finds out who I am it'll all start again, especially if Carrie gets released."

Her face sank into a pleading expression as she leaned forward to clutch his hands in hers.

"Please Ethan, I beg you. Don't recommend parole for Carrie Martins, it's too soon, too raw for her victims. We've never had closure because that bitch won't tell us where the children are, she can't just walk away from that into a new life with a new identity."

Ethan sighed, he completely understood her impassioned plea but he had to stay objective. At the moment he was leaning towards not recommending parole, but he couldn't let his opinion be coloured by May's personal feelings.

"All I can say is that I'll be writing a report that's as accurate as I can. I know what factors to take into account and her lack of remorse is a big part of that."

Although he hadn't agreed with her, May did look less fraught and nodded her thanks.

"I appreciate that Ethan, and I'll take on board what you said about telling Dr Edwards. I've just got to build up my courage to share it with him, I've kept it hidden so long it's second nature to keep it to myself."

After she left Ethan stared at the wall while he put his thoughts in order. He didn't feel entirely comfortable keeping May's secret. If Jim found out he'd known and not said anything he'd be in as much trouble as her, if not more.

Every time Ethan ran into May that day, she threw him a sad, pleading look that made him feel like a shitty person. It was no good though, he couldn't keep her secret and he knew he had to be up front and give her an ultimatum. His opportunity came when they ran into each other in the staff kitchen. May was making herself a mint tea and the smell made him fancy the same thing. He reached up for a mug and added one of the bags trying to think about how he could word what he was about to say to her.

The silence hung heavy and uncomfortable, but it was May who spoke first in the end.

"I'm just having this and then I'm going to see Dr Edwards before my nerve goes. Thank you for not running straight to him and for giving me time to make the choice myself."

Ethan blew on the top of his drink and tried to find some reassuring words for her.

"I'll never know how hard it must be for you, but you're doing the right thing. You shouldn't have to work with Carrie Martins, it must be destroying you every time you have to deal with her."

May nodded, "I'd got to a point where I was pushing all my emotions down and locking them away so I could do my job. I had no idea how badly that was effecting me until you called me out. I've spent all morning going over it, and I can see that I wasn't coping as well as I was making out."

Although it still felt awkward, and May was clearly a bundle of nerves, Ethan like that they'd cleared the air. He wasn't sure what Dr Edwards would do in response to May's disclosure, but he hoped it didn't affect her job at the prison. Surely he'd just transfer her to another wing?

It wasn't long until Ethan found out. He'd just stepped out of his office when he heard the sound of a door slamming. Looking around he spotted May, her eyes red rimmed and her hands clenched into fists as she stormed down the corridor. Ethan reached out to try and get her attention and she whirled around to face him.

"I've lost my job."

Ethan shook his head in disbelief, "He sacked you on the spot?"

May sniffed loudly, "He may as well have done. Apparently I'm suspended while the prison investigates and if they find that I'm in breach of policy or my deception affected Carrie Martins I'll face a hearing. Dismissal is still on the table, Jim told me to make sure I get a union rep."

He knew that Jim probably didn't have much choice in how he handled it. This was a potentially serious situation, a family member of a victim was working with the woman convicted of their murder. If it got out there'd be a scandal about how good the checks were before someone started work here. Knowing it was inevitable wouldn't help May, she loved her job and now she was facing losing everything.

"I hate that bitch. If there's anything good to come out of this, it's that I don't have to see Carrie Martins's smug face ever again."

With that final comment spat at Ethan, May strode down the corridor and out of the wing.

Cal had proved indispensable yet again by finding Monica Hayes and persuading her to speak to them. She'd agreed to meet them at a wine bar near her home and had stalked in ten minutes after they'd arrived. She looked around until her eyes alighted on their table. Clearly working out they were the people she was meeting she got herself a large white wine before joining them.

Monica looked like the stereotype of a primary teacher. Her blonde hair was cut sensibly short and the curls framed a face that looked kind even through her serious expression. She swirled the wine in her glass and looked thoughtfully at the table before speaking.

"I've probably run this through my head a hundred times over the years, especially after Carrie was arrested. I've asked myself if there was something I missed but I can't see how anyone could've known she was a cold-blooded killer. Those poor children were in my class, she sat with them and knew them."

Monica shuddered, "The thought of her being so cold that she could kill a child she knew and was close to makes me feel sick."

Cal nodded, "That always struck me as well. The papers made a good point when they called her the Child Catcher. It summed it up really."

Having someone back up her thought process seemed to give Monica permission to continue because, after a gulp of wine, she launched into the story.

"Carrie was one of only four applicants for the job. Two of them were clearly unsuitable so it came down to a choice between her and a woman I'd encouraged to apply. I know that when I first raised concerns about her a lot of people thought it was sour grapes but it wasn't. From her first day, Carrie wasn't the person we'd met at her interview, she strolled in over half an hour late and didn't give a single shit. No apology or excuse, she just dumped off her coat and waited to be told what to do. It went downhill from there really. Carrie's main responsibility was working with the more challenging children in the class, but she preferred the ones that were easier to work with. I had to constantly remind her to help the children that were struggling the most and she'd take on this sulky look like a child deprived of a treat. She worked a lot with Tessie and Emily. They were lovely children, always smiling and keen to work. That made them ideal from Carrie's perspective, why push an unwilling child when you could have an easy day with those who enjoyed reading? I raised it with the head, but on the day he came to class to observe she was completely different and he brushed off my complaints. I tried all different ways of approaching her, but she just set herself against my orders and did what she wanted anyway. It was becoming intolerable, and after a particularly difficult morning, I called her to one side and was blunt about how she wasn't meeting my expectations. I'll never forget how hateful the look was that she gave me before storming out of the classroom. She didn't return before break time and to be honest, I enjoyed having her out of the room so I didn't go look for her. I wish I had now because it was Emily and Tessie who found her supposedly crying in the bathrooms. She told them I'd said something really horrible to her, and when they came back I could tell they weren't happy with me. Carrie kept giving me smug, sly looks and I just knew she'd said something to the girls. The headmaster spoke to her about it and he said he was very clear about the risk to her probation. After that I had a few incidents that looking back make me wonder if Carrie wasn't behind them. Someone keyed my new car and tipped paint stripper on the boot. Then cat poo turned up on my doorstep, and someone posted dog shit through my letterbox. My boyfriend thought I was overreacting and it was just kids messing about, but I had a horrible feeling it was Carrie paying me back."

Monica leaned back in her chair, "I did confront her about it at one point. She gave me a smug look as she denied it. I can still hear what she said too. "That sounds awful Miss Hayes. You haven't upset anyone have you?" I couldn't prove it was her, but I knew it was. I'd like to say I was completely shocked by what happened, but having seen the way Carrie was it all had a terrible sense of inevitability about it. She was unstable, I could tell that from the way she behaved, and she should never have been around small children."

Ethan couldn't help but think that this was a great hindsight observation, typical of people who think they missed something important.

As a teacher, and not just any teacher, their teacher, she was bound to have spent a lot of time going back and forth over it all. It must've been devastating to not only have three children from your class murdered but to have known that their killer was working with you every day beforehand.

The truth was no one could predict something like this, psychopaths could kill for no more reason than someone spilling coffee on their shirt. It was interesting though how once again Carrie's version of events just didn't match up with how it was seen through someone else's eyes. Was it just a matter of perspective, or was Carrie the cold liar everyone had told him she was?

Chapter Twenty Six

The email waiting in his inbox first thing was from Dr Edwards.

It was a "gentle reminder" that he hadn't given him any further updates on his report, and that he should be thinking about completing it soon. He'd also updated on May's suspension and investigation pointing out that Ethan would need to give a statement. Ethan leaned back in his chair and thought about where he'd got to with it all. He had the bones of a report. The lies, the deception, the lack of taking responsibility, all those added up to her being unsuited for parole. It would be the easiest thing in the world to just create his report based on that, but Ethan sensed there was more to it. He wasn't a man who just did the bare minimum, and he didn't feel right putting anything official together until he knew all the facts.

What about Dan's role? Had her brother taken part in the murders or even worse been the one to commit them? Had Carrie taken the blame for him? On the surface, they didn't have a close relationship but was that how she wanted him to see it? If no one thought they were close no one would suspect she was covering for him. He got a place in a secure hospital, and Carrie took the prison time. It didn't hold a ring of truth for him, but considering how good she was at showing the face she wanted people to see it wasn't impossible either.

Then there was Carrie's dad, he was a man who always seemed to be hiding who he really was. Guarded and suspicious were words that sprang to mind when you thought about Stan. Was that to protect his privacy as he said it was, or was it really to hide what he'd done? Ethan had a sense of Carrie holding back about her dad, and it made him wonder what secrets they were hiding.

On top of that, he was sad about May's suspension. He was also nervous on his own behalf about giving a statement for her hearing. What was he supposed to say? Anything he put in it would likely nail the final door shut for her, plus he had his own bending of the rules to hide. What if Jim started poking around and found out about his use of the system to find Dan and Mandy Martins? What if they discovered he was meeting with a journalist and digging about in a patient's personal history?

There was only one way to resolve this, he needed to see Carrie and tell her exactly what was at stake. If she didn't start opening up there was no way he could clear her for parole, the risk was too high. If everything came out and he ended up joining May on suspension he wanted to get this case closed before that happened.

Ethan could see he'd thrown Carrie by the surprise session. It made him realise that the planning usually involved played into her hands and allowed her to prepare what face she wanted to show him. Maybe this time he'd get something more honest from her. Carrie's eyes strayed to the camera blinking in the corner of the room before she shifted awkwardly on her chair.

"Carrie, I need to be upfront with you. The way things stand there's no way I can give you a report that supports parole. The risk is too high considering you aren't willing to open up to me."

Her eyes darted around the room as she took in his unusual bluntness. It was time to take the gloves off and see where things fell. If he didn't push her buttons now when she had something to gain from opening up then instinct told him he'd never get to the truth.

Carrie sighed and chewed her lip. This was a new Carrie, a combination of all the faces she'd shown him before.

"He'll kill me if I tell. He said he would and I know he'd do it."

Ethan waited her out, if he jumped in now she'd clam up and he'd get nothing more. Without knowing who "he" was there was no way of reassuring her anyway.

"If I tell you, then you have to protect me. Promise you'll do everything you can to make sure I'm safe, and in return, I'll tell you the truth."

Ethan nodded, it was easy to agree to as he'd never leave anyone at risk if it was within his power to help. Carrie seemed mollified by his agreeance and settled back to tell him the last part of her story.

Chapter
Twenty-Seven

Carrie

The girls loved fairies.

I'm sure most children have a fascination with the fantasy world, but Tessie and Emily were completely enraptured by them. I loved it, we created beautiful stories and they drew lovely pictures. It was the Friday before half-term when they told me they'd heard there was a fairy ring in the woods. Apparently, someone had told them that under the oldest oak tree in the clearing, they'd find fairy toadstools. Tessie told me they were planning to sneak up there after school and I decided it would be better if an adult went along. I offered to join them, and as I'd proved myself to be a fellow fairy fan they quickly agreed. I let my father know I might be late home for tea and why and then set off as soon as I could get away from work.

We met at the entrance to the woods. Emily and Tessie had brought their friend Thomas with them so with all three children in tow we set off to find fairy toadstools. It was lovely, the children and I wove stories as we walked and it cast a certain aura of magic over us all.

I'd had a terrible term and this was just the balm I needed to make me feel as though it was all worth it. I'd made a connection with these three children and it proved Monica wrong, I wasn't a terrible teaching assistant at all. Tessie and Emily held one of my hands each and Thomas lagged behind us, kicking leaves and generally being a mischievous boy. I hold on to those images, those are the memories I use to hide behind so I don't have to see what happened later. It doesn't always work though, all too often the nightmares creep in and I see what happened over and over again.

Anyway, I digress.

The tree looked magical, spider webs sparkled from its branches, and the light through the canopy of leaves above us created a golden glow. As we started searching for the toadstools I heard Tessie scream. Just the once, before it was sharply cut off as though something, or someone, had stopped her. I spun around and there was my father looking down the steep embankment. Running over to see what had happened I immediately saw Tessie lying at the bottom. She was still and unmoving, and her head was twisted at such an unnatural angle I was immediately certain she was dead.

My father didn't seem concerned and by now the other two children had joined us. As soon as they spotted Tessie they panicked, Emily screamed and I put my hand over her mouth to stop her. My father gets very upset by loud noises and I was still hoping we could salvage the situation. I should've known better, my father was angry, as angry as I'd seen him for a long time.

"They should've kept their mouths shut. Telling tales and getting you into trouble like that. They need to learn their lesson."

I knew then that Emily and Thomas were in danger too. I had to try and get them to run away, but my father grabbed both children by their arms. I didn't want to look, but I was frozen to the spot as he threw them both over the embankment. He didn't flinch or hesitate, he just swung them over the edge as though they were bags of rubbish he was disposing of. His face was cold and cruel. I heard the dull thuds as their little bodies hit the ground and I only just stopped myself from throwing up.

"Go home, Carrie. There's no need for you to see anymore, leave your Daddy to deal with it. Daddy knows best."

I wanted to argue, to climb down and see if I could save them somehow, but years of obeying my father won out so I turned around and walked out of those woods alone.

When I got home I started to wonder if I'd imagined it. Surely my father hadn't really thrown three children to their deaths for no more reason than to punish them for telling tales about me? It must've been a horrible nightmare. My clothes were covered in twigs and leaves from running through the woods to get away, but it was almost as though I was in some sort of stupor. I had a shower, put on fresh clothes, and dumped the dirty ones in the laundry basket. I'd pushed the whole thing out of my head by that time. All I was thinking about was what to cook Daddy for his dinner. I was late starting it and he'd be home soon and mad at me for getting nothing ready.

It's the silly little things that stand out the most. Like looking in the fridge and finding there was no minced beef to make a cottage pie. Then I was emptying the freezer hunting for something suitable that wouldn't need hours to defrost. Dad came home to find me on the floor surrounded by half-empty packs of peas and carrots and holding a tub I'd found in there as I tried to work out if it was butternut squash soup or meatballs in sauce.

He didn't mention a word of what had happened earlier. He just took the tub out of my hands and put everything back in the freezer.

"Let's just get a takeout, shall we? We work hard enough to justify a treat every now and again. What do you fancy? Curry? Pizza?"

I remember clearly that we had a curry. Dad overordered and the table was strewn with far too much food. We ate it again the next night and I think there was even enough for Dad to have it on the third day too. Dan barely ate anything. Dad had forced him to sit at the table with us and the poor boy had his head bowed low and he pushed the food around his plate. In the end, Daddy lost his temper and told him to fuck off to his room.

"Your sour little face is putting me off my dinner."

It was then that I started to wonder what Dan had seen, but it wasn't until later that I realised he'd witnessed it all.

I totally wiped it from my mind overnight. I got up the next morning and was as shocked as everyone else when I saw the news that the kids were missing. I didn't remember any of it, not going into the woods, what my father did to them, nothing at all.

It was as though the whole thing hadn't happened and I just carried on day to day as normal. Or as normal as you can get when you're the teaching assistant in a class where three children are missing. We did our best to support the other children, but you could see the fear in their faces. Attendance was down as frightened parents kept their children under careful watch.

Our small town was full of journalists. Everywhere you went someone poked a microphone in your face and asked you to comment on the missing children. As the teaching assistant, I was very much in demand and I'd often leave school to find a whole bunch of them standing around my car waiting for me. Ignoring them didn't work, and neither did telling them to fuck off, they just persisted in digging for people to speak to. The poor families were hounded constantly,

I've never understood the need to harass and distress the parents of missing or murdered children.

To me, having blocked all the memories of that day, I was just being swept along with everyone else. When the police arrested me in the supermarket I had no idea why. Even when they said it was on suspicion of being involved in the disappearance of Tessie Connor, Thomas Jones, and Emily Little I was just thrown into a state of confusion. I dropped my shopping basket and I remember watching my groceries crash onto the floor, eggs, jam, and milk all mixed together in a sticky mess. Everyone in the shop was staring but no one said a word until the automatic doors started to close behind me.

All the way to the police station I was in shock, I just kept saying "I don't understand."

The officers weren't interested in what I did or didn't understand, to them I was a child killer who deserved no sympathy. I was booked in and thrown in a cell. Someone brought me a tepid cup of tea and a dry sandwich and I was left there until a man showed up telling me he was the duty solicitor and he'd be representing me. I had no idea what he meant, represent me for what?

He gave an impatient sigh as though I was wasting his time.

"Save the theatrics for the police and the courts Miss Martin. I need your full attention. You're being accused of killing the three children who went missing, you were seen taking them into the woods and you were later seen leaving alone. Even without any other evidence that alone is enough to raise some serious questions. Then there's Tessie Connor's shoe, blood stained and chucked into the undergrowth."

The lawyer, Mr Twine, could see I was still confused, and maybe by this time, he wasn't so sure it was an act.

"I need you to think hard Miss Martin, if you can tell the police where those children are then it'll go better for you."

I could see he was serious but I had no idea what he was talking about, why would I know where Tessie, Emily, and Thomas were? He just rolled his eyes and sighed. He smelt of stale cigars and I imagined how he'd prefer to be sat smoking one right now and not trapped in a grubby interview room with a woman who didn't seem to understand what he wanted her to do.

The rest of it was a blur. I have some stand-out sounds and images like the recording system in the interview room letting out that long bleep that seems to go on forever. The looks of disgust that the officers tried to hide behind a professionally blank expression, and how they wrote "murder" on the board outside my cell.

Court was surreal, and when the judge passed on the jury's verdict of guilty it was as though they were talking about someone else. I heard the cheers and applause as they led me down to the prison van outside. That was the start of me having to accept that this was my new life. No being a teacher, no meeting a nice man, and getting married and having children of my own. That was all over, and a small cell that stank of piss and other people's sweat was all there was for me, forever.

Chapter Twenty-Eight

"Do you know where the children are buried, Carrie?"

His question made the colour drain from her face but she nodded slowly.

"Yes, or at least I think I do."

Ethan couldn't let his mind wander too far, if he did he'd break at the thought of what happened to those children.

"Do you understand that I need to tell the authorities what you've just disclosed?"

Carrie nodded again and swallowed, she rubbed her eyes with the balls of her hands.

"Yes, and I'll help as much as I can. I know I should've spoken up before, but I was terrified of him. My memories started to come back about a year later, and I was horrified to realise what had really happened. This was how my father was my entire life and he wanted me to be the same way as him. He taught me how to punish those who did me wrong and I was so desperate for his love and approval I did everything I was told. I once hung a little girl over a hole in a building site and threatened to drop her just because she'd spilled orange juice on my favourite notebook. He was so proud of that, he told me I was his good girl. Daddy knows best. It's what he said every time he wanted me to do something I might not want to do."

Ethan knew exactly what she was referring to and for once felt fairly certain he was hearing the truth.

"Was your brother involved?"

He couldn't be sure but it looked as though her lips tugged upwards in a brief sneer before her features settled back to the expression of fear and sadness she'd worn before.

"Dan? Why, what's he told you about it?"

Interesting. Ethan was getting the feeling that she was sounding out how much Dan knew or had seen. Were there still parts of this story that weren't true?

"He's not been able to verbalise anything so far, I was just curious as to what caused him to become so unwell so rapidly."

Carrie nodded, "Poor Dan. He was always fragile. I'm really not sure, I didn't think he was there but he often followed me so I couldn't say for certain. He seemed worse afterward, but because I didn't remember anything I didn't link that with the children's disappearance."

Ethan nodded and then motioned to the guards outside the door.

"I need to make a few calls Carrie, and then either I or another member of staff will come and let you know what happens next."

She managed a watery smile, her reddened eyes looked sore and Ethan couldn't help a moment of sympathy. All those years of being called the Child Catcher and thought to be a monster when she wasn't. Stan had won himself years of freedom that he wasn't entitled to and if it hadn't been for this parole report the truth might never have come out.

So many lives were affected. Dan locked away in hospital, and even May and how she'd quite possibly lost her job. Ethan sighed, this was a huge mess, but it wasn't too late to put it right. Picking up the phone he dialed the number for DCI Greggs.

· • • ● ●· ● ● • •· ·

Stan Martins stood a short distance away from the embankment.

He was flanked on either side by two burly officers with his hands cuffed behind his back. He stoically stared forward as though avoiding meeting Carrie's frightened looks that she darted in his direction every now and again.

"I didn't realise he'd be here. I don't know if I can go through with it with him watching me."

Carrie hissed this to Ethan who gave her a reassuring pat on her shoulder.

"He's right over there and he can't get to you. The police felt we might need his input at some point, but since he's said nothing since they arrested him I'm not sure how much help he'll be."

She nodded briskly and looked back down the steep drop of the embankment. From right up here, there were no outward signs that there was anything of interest down there. The police and forensic team had arranged for the staff to be lowered down with their equipment and were currently gently sifting through the earth looking for any evidence of the children.

"The shoe was found just there."

The voice belonged to DCI Greggs, who pointed towards the base of the oak tree.

"It was just lying in the undergrowth, dirty and spotted with Tessie's blood."

Greggs gave Carrie the bog eye. Despite her assistance, the police had all treated her like a murderer rather than a witness. It seemed that believing the worst of her would take a while to filter out, thought Ethan. He understood though, he was personally finding it difficult not to read into everything she said and did too.

"Hey boss, down here!"

Greggs excused himself after giving Carrie another pointed look, she turned to Ethan and shrugged.

"I can't blame them. It's not as though I'm completely innocent, is it? I still kept quiet about what really happened, and I could've given the poor families closure so much sooner."

Before he could answer they became aware of a flurry of activity from below. Leaning over the edge they could see the tiny figures of the officers and white-suited forensic team leaning over a spot on the ground. When the tent was brought over it was obvious that they'd found something, or someone.

Carrie sniffed and wiped her eyes. The police had reluctantly agreed not to cuff her while she was here, and Ethan had volunteered to take full responsibility for her. He was pretty sure she wouldn't try to do a runner considering what was happening was likely to get her acquitted of murder.

When a scuffle broke out to his left Ethan instinctively moved in front of Carrie. It was her father fighting with the officers who were reading him his rights and dragging him toward a waiting custody van. He looked straight at Carrie whose face crumpled. She leaned around Ethan and called out to her father.

"I'm sorry Daddy, please don't hate me. I had to tell."

He gave her a look of disgust and spat on the floor letting that be his only response. Carrie broke down, her shoulders shaking with the sobs that wracked her thin frame. Ethan took her arm and helped her up.

"Come on, let's get you back to Chartridge."

Carrie stumbled along beside him and he could hear her choking back her tears. Ethan was just planning a session to help her come to terms with all of this when he rounded the corner and realised that the field they'd come into the woods through was now full of people.

Not just any people either, journalists. Everyone was focused on the woods, tv news crews, photographers, and members of the public had all converged on the scene.

"Who the fuck has been leaking information?"

DCI Greggs had caught them up and was staring at the scene ahead in horror.

"That's all we fucking need, a picture of the Child Catcher on the front pages opening all of this up before we get a chance to investigate."

Carrie winced at the use of her media-generated nickname but didn't say anything. Greggs turned to give Ethan a long, suspicious stare.

"I didn't say anything. I hardly want to feature on the front pages either."

DCI Greggs must've decided that made sense because he turned away and called out to a uniform that was loitering nearby.

"Potts, I want to know the name and rank of every officer involved today. I will keep digging until I find out who told that bunch of vultures what was going down here."

Potts swallowed hard at the edge of his boss's voice before quickly heading back toward the crime scene. Ethan stood in front of Carrie sheltering her from anyone who might be able to pick her out using their long lens cameras.

DCI Greggs sighed, "We're going to have to think of a way to get her out of here without anyone seeing. I'll get our press officer to let them know we'll be making a statement in half an hour. That'll hold them for a bit while we try to come up with a plan."

He looked around thoughtfully until he spotted one of the forensic officers walking back lugging some equipment. Holding up a hand to indicate that Ethan and Carrie should stay put he hurried over. After a brief whispered conversation, he came back holding something in his arms that he held out to Carrie.

"Put these on. It's a forensic suit, pull the hood over and make it tight so you can only just see out. We'll then all walk out together as though we're part of the team. They'll try to call out questions so everyone ignore them and don't even look up. They won't follow because they won't want to lose their spot for the statement."

Carrie pulled the suit over her clothes. It was a little baggy on her thin frame but that worked in her favour as the hood flopped over her face enough to hide who she was. They stepped out from their sanctuary behind the trees, and as DCI Greggs had predicted loud voices shouted questions toward them.

"Have you found a body?"

"Is it the Child Catcher's victims?"

"Do the families know about this?"

The party of three kept their faces turned away and closed their ears to the bombardment of shouts and questions. Ethan could feel Carrie trembling as she brushed against his arm and he was relieved when they finally got to his car.

DCI Greggs leaned against the driver's door as Ethan was about to climb in.

"I'm going to need to talk to you later. I'll call when I can get away from here."

With a knowing nod in Ethan's direction, he headed back to the woods and was soon lost in the crowd of shouting journalists again.

Chapter Twenty-Nine

The papers had run with what they had.

The articles were light on facts and heavy on conjecture, but they all had the same result. A renewed interest in the Child Catcher. Whoever leaked the police operation yesterday either hadn't had access to many details or held them back as no one was aware of Stan Martin's arrest yet.

Ethan was still processing it all. Carrie was due to be released while the courts considered dropping her murder conviction and reducing it to the lesser charge of assisting an offender. That would mean time served applied and she'd be effectively free to go. Ethan had taken the day off work to meet with DCI Greggs and find out what he wanted to talk to him about. Now he was sat here his mind racing with questions as he considered what the detective had told him.

They'd met at Ethan's house, and after making Greggs a coffee and putting out the biscuit tin, the police officer explained what was still bothering him about the case.

"It's not as cut and dried as it's being made out to be. Why is no one interested in the physical evidence anymore? That shoe we found was in the undergrowth under that big tree, it was filthy and had spots of Tessie's blood all over it. So, if she fell or was pushed over the embankment how would she have lost her shoe first? Where did the blood come from?"

Ethan had thought for a moment, it didn't entirely make sense to him either, but he stretched for a logical explanation.

"Could be that she lost her shoe or that it dropped off when Stan grabbed her. Maybe she had a nosebleed or cut her knee? We'll never know and I'd guess it isn't enough to re-open the case."

Greggs shrugged, his face a picture of frustration, "I don't like loose ends Doc, and this is a loose end. That woman has lied and lied, and lied again, what makes anyone think she's telling the truth now?"

That was the sentence that rang in Ethan's ears, and the one that was echoing now as he tried to convince himself he hadn't just made the biggest mistake of his life. He also wasn't a fan of loose ends, and one that had kept bugging him was Dan. What was his role in all of this? Was he the only person who knew the real truth behind what happened that day in the woods?

Mandy was waiting for him at the access gates to the hospital. She looked as though she was deciding whether to stay or make a run for it. Ethan gave her a reassuring smile as he approached.

"It's fine if you don't feel ready, we can do this another day when you feel stronger."

She shook her head and jutted out her chin giving her the air of a stubborn child.

"No. I'm ready, more than ready, to see my son. It's been too long already."

Ethan led her into the hospital where Stella was waiting to greet them and take them to the secure floor. In the lift, she gently prepared Mandy for what she'd find.

"He's been more responsive lately, but he's mostly nonverbal. Don't be surprised if he doesn't act pleased to see you and shows no interest in you, that's just how he is. If you look closely enough you might be able to read what he's really thinking, but he tends to keep a tight lid on himself."

That didn't stop Mandy from gasping when she went into his room and saw the reality for herself. To Ethan, Dan looked better. He was dressed, his hair had been trimmed and brushed, and he shot the odd look in their direction. He wasn't aggressively scribbling pictures on paper today either, Ethan noticed, but for his mum, it was still a sad sight.

Mandy twiddled her thumbs anxiously, clearly unsure what to do, so Ethan prompted her to go and greet her son.

"Just speak to him gently and see where it goes from there. I'll stay out of the way and give you guys your space."

She approached him tentatively. Her hand outstretched to touch him, and then she pulled away at the moment she'd have made contact. Dan leaned very slightly toward her which Ethan saw as a positive. Turning away from mother and son he found himself looking at the strip of pictures that did a full circuit around the walls.

Knowing what he did now he realised where the starting point was. The one by the door showed a taller stick figure leading 3 smaller ones into the trees. Following the images Ethan began to see how Dan had created the whole story. Reaching the one that appeared to depict Stan, he frowned and went back to the one before. Darting his eyes between the two he tried to take in what it was saying to him. Maybe Dan had got them the wrong way around?

Ethan continued along and read Dan's depiction of what he'd seen, and then went back and did the same route again. When he looked up it was to see Dan watching him intently. Instead of looking through him or around him, Dan was staring directly at Ethan. His eyes were brighter than he'd seen on his previous visits. He seemed to be telling Ethan that he'd got it right, but surely he was overthinking this. Dan was a young man with a very significant diagnosis, his mind muddled by schizophrenia and powerful antipsychotics.

Dan's small nod suggested that he knew exactly what Ethan was seeing, and his stomach clenched as he realised what the truth was.

There was only one person who could clear this up, Stanley Martins.

He was being held in custody awaiting his trial, and due to Ethan's position at HMP Chartridge, he was able to pull a few strings and get himself a professional visit.

Stan strode into the room with a swagger that suggested he could handle himself. No more than a day in custody and he'd already taken on the don't mess with me image that he felt would keep him safe. Dragging out the chair opposite he threw himself down and eyed Ethan with open hostility. Once the officers had left the room Stan let himself relax, and then surprisingly burst into gales of laughter.

"Your face! I can read it a mile off. You've worked out that she had you over, haven't you?"

Ethan waited until he'd finished chuckling to himself, "I'm not sure why it's funny Mr Martins. Three children are dead regardless of who did what, and it's you and your daughter who did it."

Stan narrowed his eyes, "That girl was always a wrong 'un. I did my best after that useless bitch that birthed her left, but she had a cruel streak a mile wide. One time she was so pissed at her friend's little sister for spilling juice on her favourite notebook she held her over a hole at a building site and threatened to drop her. It took some cleaning up on my part to get her out of that I can tell you. She was always at it, hurting other children and doing spiteful things to pay people back when they slighted her. And it didn't take much either. Carrie was always ready to take offence and woe betide if you got on the wrong side of her."

Ethan could see the man was taking pleasure in smugly telling him where he'd gone wrong. The problem was, Ethan still couldn't be sure who to believe anymore.

"Then tell me your version of what really happened that day in the woods."

Stan snorted, "Okay, but it's up to you what you want to believe at the end of it. I knew she was pissed at those girls, she'd come home fuming about how they'd told tales about her to that bitch teacher Monica. When she said she was meeting them for some kind of weird fairy hunt I knew there was more to it. She had that look on her face that she got when she was about to do something really terrible, sort of dreamy as though she was enjoying picturing it in her head. Anyway, I snuck over there and got to the tree too late. She'd already shoved those poor kids over the embankment. It was a massive drop, with branches and rocks jutting out from all sides. No way anyone would survive it, let alone a small child. Carrie was leaning over the edge and smiling to herself. I was tempted to shove her over, but instead, I looked down too. I wish I hadn't. Those poor kiddies were all crumpled up on the ground below and I knew they were dead. Carrie was laughing by now, so I told the sick bitch to fuck off home while I sorted it. That was always my role, stepping in and cleaning up her messes. She went, and I got some ropes and shit out of my van, and lowered myself down to the bottom. I buried them right there, and then I had to get myself all the way back up the same way I went down. Nearly bloody killed me doing it, and then she repaid me by dumping the blame on me. Fucking marvelous."

Stan shook his head, "Later that night she told me they'd deserved it. Cold as ice she just thanked me for helping, and then the next morning it was as though it hadn't happened. She even kept updating me as though we were watching it unfold like the rest of the town. She's more mental than my lad. I was actually relieved when she got arrested and the charges stuck. God knows what she did to that lassie before she killed her either. When I heard about the blood in her shoe I felt physically sick."

The whole story made horrible sense to Ethan, but there was still one extra part that he needed to know.

"And what about Dan? Did he see it all?"

Stan rolled his eyes, "Stupid kid followed Carrie everywhere like a kicked puppy desperate for her affection. I didn't know he'd seen it all until I caught a glimpse of him running off when I got back up the embankment that night. A few weeks later I found him rocking back and forth in his room. He'd drawn all this crazy shit on the walls and wouldn't say a word. I got a doctor to come out and he recommended putting him in hospital. What else could I do? Best place for him really, at least he couldn't spill the beans on what really happened."

"Why didn't you say anything at the time?"

Tapping his fingers on the table he leveled a look at Ethan that suggested he thought he was thick.

"Yeah, and I'd have been in the shit too for helping her. I had no choice but to keep my mouth shut, and if she'd shut up we'd all be alright wouldn't we? But no, Carrie wanted out at any cost and here we are."

Chapter Thirty

C arrie had been packing up her belongings when Ethan had summoned her to one last session.

Rachel had given a slightly smug smile at the thought of interrupting her, but Carrie was full of the joys of "blowing this joint," as she put it when she came through the door.

"Hi Doc, what gives?"

She threw herself in the chair and smiled happily at him, a smile that dropped away when she heard what he had to say.

"I had an interesting conversation with your dad yesterday, and your brother's pictures tell a very different story to the one you told me."

There was a flare of anger that danced across her face and added a hard edge that made him shudder. In that brief moment, he saw the monster beneath the masks and he hoped not to see it again. She tucked it away and replaced it with the carefree expression of happiness that she'd been wearing when she came in earlier.

"My Daddy is a liar, he always has been, and always will be. I expect he's desperately trying to put the blame back on me to get himself out of trouble."

Ethan smiled at her, "And what about Dan's pictures? How do you explain those? They clearly show you being the perpetrator and not your dad."

Carrie laughed and shook her head, "That mental idiot, who'll take any notice of anything he says. He's spent his whole adult life in a facility, he's got no credibility. Forget it, Ethan, your job's done and I've got my release. Best we leave it at that."

"I'm not the sort of person to just walk away from an injustice Carrie. You should know that better than anyone because wasn't that why you picked me to play your games with?"

She smirked, "Go ahead, shout it from the rooftops, see if I care. You got me released and now you want to take it back, how will that look? It'll just feed into all the people who said you were getting too involved in my case. I heard the officers talking, they all said you weren't objective enough when it came to me."

Ethan could feel his temper rising, "I don't care about any of that, I'll do what's right regardless."

Carrie just shrugged, "I'm a brilliant actress, Ethan, you must've noticed how good I am. I'll turn on the waterworks and tell them how you were making sexual demands, and when I said no this is how you paid me back. I'll ruin you, your career will be in tatters, and you'll have nothing left. Is that what you want?"

Drumming her fingers on the tabletop she gave him a cold smile of triumph.

"Actually, that's an interesting narrative. Maybe Dan was the one to help Dad after I left and that's why he had the breakdown. Hmm, yes, I like it. That'll keep the little idiot out of my business permanently."

Forcing down his annoyance, Ethan gave her a smile as though he wasn't bothered in the slightest.

"Since we're in honesty corner, I'd like to know more about what happened to Olive and Pepper. Were the staff right about your involvement?"

Carrie smirked and snorted with laughter, but he noticed she double-checked that the camera was off before she answered him. Seeing no red light blinking to show it was recording she looked him in the eye.

"Olive was an idiot. I'm sure you can't imagine how much fun it was to play with her. Not as much fun as it would've been if she'd been a challenge, but you take what you can get. A few simple suggestions and Olive was putty in my hands. Now, Lisa, she was far more interesting. Not the brightest star in the sky, but street smart enough to be suspicious of me. I enjoyed that a lot more than Olive. Did you see the mess she made of that fat bitch's face? I was hoping for serious injury, but to get an actual death was brilliant."

Ethan masked his disgust well enough that she didn't pick up on it, but inside his stomach was churning.

"Why was there blood in Tessie's shoe?"

Carrie shook her head, "I can't believe my Dad missed that shoe. Surely he noticed that the child was only wearing one when he buried her? The blood was because I had to hit her in the face with a branch. Horrible little fighter she was. Her shoe came off in the scuffle, and she must've dripped blood in it before I dragged her to the embankment."

Ethan tried to push away the image that description had put in his head.

"Do you feel any remorse for what happened?"

She looked him up and down as though weighing him up.

"I'm sure you'd love to hear how sorry I am. Maybe it would make you feel better for falling for my stories, but the answer is no. Those girls signed their death warrants when they tried to get me fired, and poor Thomas was their fault. If they hadn't dragged him along he'd be a 22-year-old man now, I had no beef with him."

Ethan dug in his bag and dropped that morning's paper on the desk between them, he spun it around so Carrie could read the headline.

"A friend of mine wrote this up, and it's not the last one he'll be doing either. He's tenacious, and he'll keep digging up shit on you until something sticks and you're back where you belong. Enjoy your taste of freedom because I guarantee it'll be short-lived."

Pushing the paper toward her, he stood up, "I'll just leave this with you. Have a good read and consider the impact I can have on your life. I'm not the only one either, DCI Greggs is very interested in finding out what caused Tessie to lose her shoe before she even got to the embankment. He wants to know why there was blood inside them and he's another man who won't just give up and walk away."

Carrie screwed the paper up and threw it childishly across the room as Ethan laughed at her.

"Temper, temper. You wouldn't want the guards to come back in and have to manage your behaviour, would you? Might delay your release."

Carrie narrowed her eyes, but then a smile broke out across her face and she shook her head as though despairing of the actions of an annoying child.

"I'm sure you'd like to think that you can be a thorn in my side, but what have you really got apart from empty threats? Besides, you appear to be forgetting what happens to people who cross me. Be careful Ethan, I'll be out and free to do as I wish in a few short hours."

At the door, he turned for one last look at her, "You do know that there'll be another court case don't you? I'm sure you feel confident about lying to the court, but what happens if there's new evidence that doesn't support your version of events?"

Ethan didn't wait for a response, but he could hear her screaming obscenities as he strolled down the corridor. She might have won the battle, but not the war, he thought as he pushed open the main exit and walked into the sunshine. As for her threats, well, he had that stitched up too, and she'd just played right into his hands.

Just outside the gates, DCI Greggs was patiently waiting for him, Ethan gave him a nod and the detective punched the air in victory.

"So, the camera trick worked then?"

Ethan smiled, "Yep, like a dream. I didn't tell her it was off, but she checked for the red light and when she didn't see one she was happy to talk about everything."

"Perfect, it's not entrapment, and since you told her from the start that all your sessions are recorded she won't have a leg to stand on when she tries to get it dismissed from evidence."

DCI Greggs was clearly chomping at the bit to get on with the next part of their plan. Ethan handed him the memory stick that contained the video of his earlier conversation with Carrie. It would prove, in her own words, that she'd not only killed those children but had also caused the incidents with Olive and Pepper. Ethan was hopeful that meant Lisa would get an easier ride in court.

He hadn't said anything to Carrie, but Dan was coming on in leaps and bounds. His mum was back in his life and Dan was talking again. He had a lot to say for himself too. Apparently, Carrie had threatened to kill him if he talked and he was so scared that he'd started to get paranoid. Eventually, he'd closed down completely and that had allowed Stan to stash him away in hospital. He was now feeling confident enough to make a statement about what he'd seen that day and the threats Carrie had made. Carrie was finished, she just didn't know it yet. Ethan would've liked to be a fly on the wall when she found out what he'd done, but this was his last day at the prison.

In closing down Carrie's release he'd also come to the conclusion that this wasn't the role for him. Stella had sent him an application form and he was starting his new job at the hospital in a month's time. In between he was going to take a break and finalise his divorce. May was likely to get away with a slap on the wrist and he'd been working on her following him to his new job. Deception aside, she was a great nurse who was now finding her past turmoil eased by the revelations he'd uncovered. Ethan had also decided he was going to make his house into a home, starting with adopting a cat.

He watched DCI Greggs as he strode into the prison ready to make sure that Carrie never saw the light of day again. Ethan smiled to himself as he realised what the time was. He needed to get a move on, he had an appointment to meet Stella at the local cattery. There was a beautiful young cat looking for a new home, and Ethan had decided he needed to reach out and be less alone.

Also By - Molly Garcia

Psychological Thrillers:

One Blue Shoe
The Love of His Life
Still The Love of His Life
Always The Love of His Life

Supernatural Thrillers:

Willow Weeps
Save Us

Horror

Greed Box
Tales of Darkness Drive
Comeuppance